G.J. KEMP

THE ACRE SERIES

Valen and the Beasts
(A Juno and the Lady Novella Book 1.1)

This edition published in 2022 by TB5 Publishing
Copyright © G.J. Kemp 2021
gjkemp.co.uk

ISBN 978-1-915379-03-0 (paperback)
ISBN 978-1-915379-04-7 (ebook)

for a boys best friend,
Jocko

ACKNOWLEDGMENTS

Right from the start, I have had a soft spot for Valen. Some of my readers have expressed the same, so this book is for you. I hope you enjoy Valen's journey.

To my incredible team who have worked tirelessly to get this novella out. Jess and Isabelle, for your guidance. My beta readers, Nanna and Lara. My editors, Claire from Cherry Edits and Andy from The Narrative Craft. Andrei for your wonderful cover. And Latifa (@latifahdesign) for all your design work.

Thank you.

THE ACRE SERIES

Thank you for your interest in The Acre Series. I recommend you read the principal novels in order as the characters and the story grow with the series. The novellas are prequels and sequels to the principal novels. You can read them in any order you wish.

—

The Acre Series

Juno and the Lady (An Acre Story Book 1)
Valen and the Beasts: A Juno and the Lady Novella (An Acre Story Book 1.1)

CHAPTER I
ARTS AND CRAFTS

The shop bell tinkled furiously as Valen nearly ripped the door off its hinges. He stepped out into the morning sunlight and stretched.

'Boo,' a young girl said, jumping out of the nearby alley.

Valen jumped up as he feigned fright. 'I should have known you would be waiting. I see you are wearing your boy clothes again.'

'Shh,' Gracie said. 'Don't say it too loud. If the guards catch me, I will go to jail.'

Valen tousled her hair. 'We are at the back end of the weaving district, Gracie. Nobody is here.'

Gracie grinned. 'What are you doing today?'

'I have to go to Bren's shop to buy some materials for my beast creations and then go off to the market to get food.'

'Ohh,' Gracie said, hopping from foot to foot. 'Can I come with you? Can I please?'

'Of course, but you know the deal. If guards get close by, get out of there.'

'I will,' Gracie said, darting into the alley, then jumping back out. 'And you need to remember that I am a boy. OK?'

With a sigh, Valen gave Gracie a thumbs-up. 'I will remember, although I don't like how you need to pretend to be a boy.'

'I don't want to pretend,' Gracie said with a sage nod. 'I have to pretend.'

'Yes, I suppose you do,' Valen said. 'Come on then, I want to get back here before lunch as I have work to do.'

They walked through the quiet streets of the weaving district until they heard the familiar thump of the loom. The new building housed the latest equipment to make the finest clothes that money could buy. Fairacre supplied the City of Lynn with food and clothes. They turned into a long winding street that led to the main east–west road that ran the length of Fairacre.

'Hey, outsider,' a man shouted from a store doorway. 'About time you bought yourself a wife, eh?'

Valen bit his bottom lip and gave the man a look of disdain.

'Who is the boy?' the man said. 'Is he your boy?'

'My friend's boy,' Valen said, straightening his back and raising himself to his full height. 'He is spending the day with me and I won't be having any trouble with you. Do you hear me?'

The man took in Valen's enormous size, then spat into the ground. 'About time you got yourself your own woman and your own boy, outsider. You understand the rules. If you don't have a wife, you have to leave the town. Hargreaves and the Captain say so.'

With a curled lip, Valen increased his stride. Up ahead, the hustle and bustle of the main road grew louder.

Gracie hopped and skipped beside him just to keep up. 'Why don't you biff him?' she said. 'A swift biff to the nose.'

'A biff, eh?' Valen said. 'And where did you find out about biffing people?'

'Naomi can biff anyone on the nose,' Gracie said, as she jabbed a flurry of punches out in front of her.

'Naomi is scary,' Valen said. 'Time to keep quiet now. We need to cross this road and get to Bren's store.'

Gracie hunched her shoulders and jammed her hands into her pockets. She hung her head, so her hair fell over the front of her face. They looked left and right, then walked across the main road.

'Hey, you there,' a guard said just as they finished crossing the road. 'Yes, you. The big man and the boy. Where are you going?'

Valen turned and narrowed his eyes at the guard. 'I am off to Bren's shop to buy supplies. Is there a reason you are stopping me?'

The guard strode over to them and sneered up into Valen's face. 'Best hold your tongue, outsider.'

Valen bit the inside of his cheek.

The guard bent over to get a better view of Gracie's face.

'He is my friend's boy,' Valen said, pulling Gracie against his thigh. 'No need to frighten the poor child now, is there?'

'You don't have any friends, outsider,' the guard spat. 'Who is he really?'

'Like I said,' Valen said, the muscles in his jaw tensing. 'He is my friend's boy.'

The guard placed a hand on his sword.

'I don't want any trouble,' Valen said, raising his other hand and softening his face. 'I would like to continue on my way.'

The guard looked up at Valen, then back down at Gracie. 'Tell your friend he shouldn't let his boy walk around with an outsider.'

'I will tell him,' Valen said.

The guard flicked his head. 'Get out of here and don't let me see you again.'

Valen and Gracie walked into the manufacturing district.

'That was close,' Gracie said. 'If he had touched me, he would have found me out.'

'I thought I said you need to disappear when the guards come,' Valen said through his teeth.

Gracie grinned at Valen. 'What, and miss all the fun? You should have biffed him. Biff, biff.'

'If I had biffed him, then a lot more guards would have biffed me. And if they caught you, you would have gone to jail and Naomi would be furious with me, and then she would have biffed me.'

'Nobody will catch me,' Gracie said, with a look of concentration. 'I am like a cat. Like an alley cat.'

'A member of the sewer rats,' Valen said. 'I thought cats and rats don't get along?'

'Oh yeah,' Gracie said. 'Well, I am a cat who likes rats. I am a sewer cat rat.'

'Sure you are,' Valen said, rolling his eyes. 'Look, we are at Bren's shop. Make sure you sit on the chair and behave yourself. Bren may look old, but he can swing that staff of his and take your head clean off.'

Gracie squared her shoulders and placed her hands behind her back. 'I shall behave, oh great one.'

Valen rattled his lips as he let out a long, drawn-out sigh. 'Just behave, OK?'

'I shall,' Gracie said, with a twinkle in her eye.

The bell that tinkled on Bren's door was not dissimilar to Valen's own. Valen closed the door behind him. 'Bren, are you home?'

'It says I am open on the door, doesn't it?' Bren said, shuffling up to the counter in the front of his shop. 'Of course I am in.'

Valen gave the old man a smile. 'You didn't turn it to closed before you went to bed, did you, old man?'

Bren picked up the first thing he could find and chucked it at Valen. 'I will take you down, boy.'

Valen swatted the scrunched-up piece of paper away from his face. 'Careful, Bren. I have a friend with me and I don't want her to get hurt.'

'And who have we here?' Bren said, bending over and squinting at Gracie.

'You have met Gracie, Bren,' Valen said, then yelped as Gracie's foot connected with his shin. 'What was that for?'

'Good evening, sir, my name is Greg,' Gracie said with an elaborate bow.

Bren snorted. 'You are going to get into trouble, Valen. If the Captain catches you with this sewer rat, it will mean jail.'

Valen curled a lip. 'Old laws in this town need to be changed.'

'Laws that say you need to buy yourself a wife, Valen. And you need to do it soon,' Bren said, wagging a finger in his face. 'I do not want my best customer thrown out of this town.'

'Let's not think of that now,' Gracie said, seeing Valen's face turn to thunder. 'We are here for some supplies, Mr Bren. Valen is building a new beast.'

'What toy you building now?' Bren said, walking around his counter.

'A snake,' Valen said. 'There are a few boys who have mentioned they would like a snake ornament in their rooms.'

Bren turned away from his counter and walked back down an aisle. 'What is it you are looking for, exactly?'

'Tubing,' Valen said. 'About as thick as Gracie's little finger.'

'Small tubing then,' Bren said while he rattled around his shelves. A moment later, he cursed, kicked a box, then disappeared through a doorway in the back.

'He is always so grumpy,' Gracie said, holding up her hands in the shape of claws. 'Grumpy and angry.'

'He has never been the same since his wife passed,' Valen said, with a sadness across his face.

'Why doesn't he just buy himself a new wife?' Gracie said, folding her arms and raising her chin.

'Don't you start,' Valen said. 'You know that makes me furious.'

Gracie unfolded her arms. 'I know. But not as angry as me.'

Valen rested both of his elbows on the counter. 'Bren's wife always made the most delicious cookies.'

'She did,' Gracie said, sitting on a chair and spinning it in a circle. 'Naomi would bring some to our home.'

'How about this?' Bren said, appearing with two hollow metal rods.

Valen took the rods and balanced them in his hand. 'These feel perfect. How much do I owe you?'

'A copper a rod,' Bren said, while frowning at the spinning Gracie. 'No more needed, as I am happy to shift the rods out of my storeroom.'

The two coins tinkled on the counter top.

'Can you stop that?' Bren said, grabbing the chair's armrest.

Gracie jumped off and pointed a tongue at Bren.

'Now, now, you two,' Valen said, pulling his bag off his back and slipping in the two rods.

'Troublemaker,' Bren said, pointing a tongue at Gracie.

'Here, put that on your back,' Valen said, handing the bag to her. 'We are off to the markets, and it might get nasty with some of those guards at the southern gate.'

'You will get kicked out of the town,' Bren mumbled. 'You shouldn't go there with this girl.'

Valen gave Bren his widest smile. 'It will be OK. Thanks for the rods, and I will see you soon, old man.'

'Call me old man again,' Bren said. 'I dare you.'

Gracie grabbed Valen by the hand and pulled him out of the

shop. 'I don't know about you, but I don't feel like getting injured today.'

Valen chuckled. 'Lead the way, my lady, I mean, my boy.'

Gracie lashed out with her shoe. Valen danced out of her way and scuttled towards the dual east–west road.

'Why are we going to the market at the southern gate?' Gracie said, catching up and walking next to Valen.

'A new delivery of food from the orchards came in this morning, and I want to get supplies for you to take to Naomi.'

'Naomi and Valen, sitting in a tree,' Gracie sang, as she skipped around Valen.

'Shh,' Valen said, cuffing Gracie around the ear. 'We are near the road and the guards will hear you.'

Gracie grinned. She stopped skipping and concentrated on walking like a boy.

As it was mid-morning, the sun sent its usual rays down the east–west road. Carts drawn by men crowded each lane. Shop owners stood outside their doors shouting what they had for sale. Valen and Gracie turned right and walked towards the centre of town. At the centre of Fairacre, the town hall and library sat in front of a large square. All around the square were houses with flat rooftops. When they reached the square, Valen and Gracie went south onto the wide cobblestone southern road. Downhill, in the distance, the towers of the southern gate rose into the sky.

'We need to be sharp and alert when we get there, Greg,' Valen said. 'Any trouble and you get down an alley and into the sewers, OK?'

This time, Gracie held her tongue as she went into full acting mode. She stooped and let her hair fall over her face. At the southern entrance of Fairacre, rows of market stalls came into view.

'I hate those two,' Gracie said, looking at the guards sitting at the gate.

'Quiet,' Valen hissed through the side of his mouth.

'The outsider has come for his groceries,' a stallholder sneered.

Valen gave the man a grim smile and inclined his head. 'A man has got to eat, sir.'

'Just make it snappy,' the vendor said.

'Maybe Bren is right,' Gracie whispered, after walking past the stall. 'Maybe it is time for you to buy your wife.'

Valen curled a lip and shook his head. 'I don't believe in buying a wife, Gracie.'

'But if you don't, they will throw you out. Then what am I and the sewer rats meant to do?'

'Let's talk about this later,' Valen said. 'You are bringing attention to us.'

Gracie glanced at the two guards who sat near the gate.

'Remember, we want four of everything,' Valen said. 'Once I pay the stallholder, make sure we get the stuff in the bag.'

Gracie swung the backpack off and loosened the drawstrings. She followed Valen up to the next stall. Stacked oranges filled each of the stall's wooden trays. Valen chatted to the owner, paid him, then signalled to Gracie. Four oversized oranges plonked into the bottom of the bag. Valen walked up to another stall, spoke, then handed a copper to the owner. Four apples joined the oranges in the bag.

'Hello, big man,' a woman said from behind the stall.

'Hello, Greta,' Valen said. 'You are out early today.'

Greta gave Valen a toothless grin. 'Got to earn my bread now, don't I, big man?'

'Stop your nattering,' the guard shouted from the gate.

Greta sneered at the guard. 'Here comes the loudmouth. Thinks he owns the place.'

The guard strode over to where they stood. He jammed his finger into Greta's face. 'You disrespected me. No food for you today.'

Greta hung her head. 'I am sorry, Mr Dec. I need some food, please.'

Dec snorted, then looked at Valen. 'And what about you? Have you chosen your wife yet? You know the Captain has his eye on you.'

Valen moved Gracie behind him. 'I am considering a few options. But today I am just here to buy food.'

Dec looked over his shoulder. 'Hey, Jon. The outsider says he is considering some options for a wife.'

'A set of women will come down from the cliffs anytime now,' Jon shouted back. 'He can have his pick.'

Valen heard Gracie mutter something.

Dec tried to peer around Valen.

'I will come and see you when the women get here, Mr Dec,' Valen said, giving him his best smile.

Dec's mouth turned into a scowl. 'You do that, eh, and I will make sure I show you the best girl. You should get a fruit picker or someone who works in the weaving shops. They can bring some money into your house.'

Valen inclined his head. 'That is a wise suggestion. I am sure you will show me the right one when the time comes.'

Dec turned to Greta. 'It looks like the outsider has improved my mood. Once you have finished sweeping, go to the stall at the end of the street. The man who owns it should have some leftovers for you.'

Greta inclined her head. 'Thank you, Mr Dec. That is very kind of you.'

Dec looked at Valen, then back at Greta, gave a nod, and strode back to the southern gate.

Valen let out a long breath. He turned and frowned at Gracie.

'I am going to kill that evil man,' Gracie whispered. 'I am going to kill him very, very slowly.'

Valen raised an eyebrow. 'That is pretty violent, Gracie.'

Gracie pouted. 'Yeah, whatever.'

'Let's continue shopping,' Valen said. 'We don't want to upset Naomi now, do we?'

'One day, I am going to be like Naomi,' Gracie said. 'She is my hero.'

With a fresh spring in his step, Valen walked off to the next market stall. His spring disappeared after the stall owner sneered at him. Four pears hit the bottom of the bag. At the next stall, another four items joined them. For the rest of the early morning, they went from market stall to market stall until Gracie struggled to hold the bag off the ground.

'Give the bag to me,' Valen said. 'You will break your shoulder trying to carry it.'

Gracie dropped the bag and huffed. 'I hate being so small.'

'Being small has its advantages,' Valen said, picking up the bag with one hand and throwing it over his shoulder. 'Come on, it is time we get back to the shop.'

'Can I come and see what you are making?' Gracie said. 'I enjoyed watching you build the bumblebee and the spider.'

Valen grinned. 'You looked more afraid than excited when I was building them.'

Gracie stood to her full height. 'I was being cautious. They are scary, you know.'

'They aren't alive,' Valen said. 'What do you think they are going to do? Pounce on you?'

Gracie skipped ahead and turned into an alley. 'Shortcut,' she said, over her shoulder. 'And if you see a live spider, you would be cautious, wouldn't you?'

Valen followed Gracie through the winding alley until they reached the road that led to the east–west road. 'Yes, I would be cautious.'

'See?' Gracie said, raising both of her hands. 'I am clever. Naomi says we should always be cautious.'

Valen smirked at Gracie as they turned south down the winding road towards the southern wall of Fairacre.

'Chosen a wife yet, son?' a man shouted through the doorway of his shop.

Valen grabbed Gracie by the scruff of the neck and propelled her forward. Gracie folded her arms and cursed colourfully at the man. They turned another corner and walked up to the front door of Valen's arts and crafts shop. The bell tinkled as Gracie pulled open the door and held it for Valen to walk through. The bell tinkled again as the door slammed shut.

Gracie barged past Valen and ran into his office. 'Whoa, is that what you are building?'

Valen walked into his office and dropped the bag on the couch. He pulled out his chair from under his office desk and sat. The chair creaked and groaned with the big man's weight.

'Yes, this is what I have been building,' Valen said, pulling the half-built metal snake closer to the end of the desk.

'He has no head,' Gracie said.

Valen reached over and pulled the two tubes out of the bag. 'I am going to make the rest of his body and his head with these tubes.'

Gracie peered at a shelf above Valen's desk. In two glass boxes, a bumblebee and a spider sat. 'Are you going to put the snake in a box like the rest?'

'I am,' Valen said. 'I am thinking of opening a new stall at the marketplace where I can sell them.'

Gracie's eyes grew wide. 'Are you sure it is safe to do that? You know the guards hate you.'

Valen ruffled Gracie's hair again. 'Dr Viktor, the man who brought me up, always said that I should keep my friends close—'

'And your enemies closer,' Gracie said, finishing his sentence. 'Naomi says that all the time.'

'So I am going to get myself closer to them so I can keep an eye on them,' Valen said. 'I am sure there are a lot of things that go on there that the mayor doesn't know about.'

Gracie nodded sagely. 'It is the one place Naomi says we need to stay away from.'

'Oh, now you tell me,' Valen said, throwing up his arms in despair. 'If she finds out, she is going to kill me.'

'Yes, Valen, you are in big trouble,' Naomi said, stepping out from the shadows.

Valen's knees banged on the bottom of his desk as he jumped with fright. His tools scattered across the desk. Gracie doubled over with laughter.

'You knew she was there all along,' Valen shouted, grabbing Gracie and tickling her.

Gracie screamed with laughter as she tried to squirm out of Valen's grip.

'Sort out the bag please, Gracie,' Naomi said, with a ghost of a smile playing on her lips. 'I need to speak to our friend here.'

'How many do I need to put in the other bag?' Gracie said, looking at Valen.

'Three of each,' Valen said. 'So leave one for me and take three for the sewer rats.'

Gracie bent over and grabbed both straps of the bag. With a grunt, she dragged it out of Valen's office and into the kitchen.

'You need to be careful when she is with you, please, Valen,'

Naomi said. 'If they catch her, she will end up at Donte's slave labour shop.'

'I promise you I will look after her,' Valen said. 'And I need to shut that man down. He is absolutely disgusting.'

Naomi raised an eyebrow. 'And how do you propose to shut him down? You know he has a lot of influence in this town.'

'I don't know how,' Valen said. 'All I know is that he is disgusting. He needs to go.'

'In a weird way, it keeps the girls off the streets because they have work,' Naomi said.

Valen snorted. 'No girl should have to sweep the streets or clean windows just so they can get a meal at the end of the day. Like you said, it's slave labour!'

'We try to save as many as we can,' Naomi said. 'But it is difficult to keep the sewer rats under the radar. The more we have, the more attention we bring to ourselves.'

'What about the mayor, Mr Hargreaves?' Valen said. 'I hear he is a reasonable man. Can't he do something about Donte?'

'Donte has links to the City of Lynn, so he has more power than Hargreaves,' Naomi said. 'Hargreaves needs to keep him happy.'

A crash of pots and pans sounded from the kitchen. 'I'm OK,' Gracie shouted.

'Stop trashing my place,' Valen shouted.

'You will make a good father one day, Valen,' Naomi said with a soft smile.

His mouth dropped open. 'Me have kids? Don't be silly.'

'Valen and Naomi, sitting in a tree,' Gracie shouted from the kitchen.

Naomi rolled her eyes. 'Shut it, you.'

Gracie burst out laughing.

'How is everything going with the sewer rats?' Valen said. 'Have you got everything you need?'

A concerned look spread across Naomi's face. 'We are running out of space. And as I mentioned, it is getting harder to keep ourselves hidden.'

'What about food?' Valen said. 'Have you got enough?'

'We are surviving,' Naomi said, looking fondly at Valen. 'You know we wouldn't have survived without your help.'

Valen waved a hand. 'It is nothing.'

'I am done,' Gracie said, dragging the bag back into the office. 'Three of everything in here.'

'Are you sure you left me some food?' Valen said. 'I am a big man who needs to eat.'

'I may have,' Gracie said, waving a hand dismissively.

'We need to get moving,' Naomi said, shaking her head at Gracie. 'The longer we stay exposed, the more dangerous it is.'

'Aw, Valen said I could watch him work on his beast,' Gracie said, her bottom lip dropping.

'It is better you come back with me,' Naomi said. 'You can always come back tomorrow.'

'She can stay with me for a few more minutes,' Valen said. 'I will make sure she gets into the alleys.'

Naomi picked up the bag. 'OK, but only a few more minutes. Remember, if you get caught, it is very hard for me to help you, Gracie.'

'Yes, ma'am,' Gracie said with a salute. 'I will make sure I head home before the sun sets.'

Naomi walked to the front door and glanced out of each window, looking for movement. The doorbell tinkled and instantly she was gone.

Gracie dragged a chair over to Valen's desk. 'What part of the snake you making?'

'His head is next,' Valen said. 'A head with red eyes and big teeth.'

'Oh yes, all scary,' Gracie said, clapping her hands. 'Have you given him a name?'

'The snake is a girl,' Valen said, swinging over an arm that held a large spyglass. 'And no, I haven't given her a name. In fact, I haven't given the other two names either.'

Gracie stared at Valen with sad eyes. 'How can you not give your beasties names?'

Valen removed the two glass boxes off the shelf and placed them on the desk in front of her. 'Well, why don't you name them then? But remember, I am just going to sell them one day so you may never see them again.'

Gracie tapped her finger on her lips. 'Hmm, what names should I give them?' she mumbled, staring out in front of her.

'Don't think too hard now,' Valen said. 'You might hurt that brain of yours.'

'Jay,' Gracie shouted, making Valen jump.

'Shh,' Valen said, waving a hand. 'We may be far from everyone here, but my neighbours can still hear you. Which one are you calling Jay?'

'The bumblebee,' Gracie said, closing one eye and looking down at the small metal bee.

'And what about the spider?' Valen said.

'I think you should name the spider,' Gracie said with a shiver. 'They freak me out.'

Valen chuckled. 'I shall call him Henry. I knew a young boy called Henry once.'

'Little Henry,' Gracie said, doing a small fist bump. 'Henry the spider, and Jay the bumblebee.'

'And what of the snake?' Valen said, picking up the snake's metal body and waving it in front of Gracie's face.

'Sia the snake,' Gracie said in a low voice. 'Snakes speak funny, so I am going to give him a name like how he speaks.'

'Oh, and you know how snakes speak, do you?' Valen said.

'Yes,' Gracie said, hissing on the letter S. 'Ssia the ssnake.'

'It is going to take me late into the night to finish Ssia, the ssnake,' Valen said. 'You can come and see her tomorrow?'

'Aw,' Gracie said. 'I hate going to the sewers.'

'I don't understand why you call your home the sewers?' Valen said. 'I promise you we will get all the girls into a nice home one day.'

Gracie opened her mouth, thought better of it, then jumped off her chair. 'I believe you. I'd best go now or Naomi will punish me.'

Valen led Gracie to the front door. 'Straight to the alley now, you hear?'

'Yes, sir,' Gracie said, saluting.

The doorbell tinkled. Gracie shot out of the shop and into the alley.

'Quick as a rat,' Valen said, closing the door behind Gracie. 'Now where was I? Oh, yes, Ssia the ssnake.'

CHAPTER 2
NAOMI

'Valen. Open up.'

'Yes, yes, stop your banging, Gracie. I am coming,' Valen said, walking down the stairs. 'The sun isn't even up yet.'

'Hurry, Valen.'

'What?' Valen said, ripping open his shop door and sending the bell tinkling. 'What do you want at this crazy hour?'

'They have caught her,' Gracie said, hopping from foot to foot. 'They have caught Naomi, Valen.'

'What do you mean, caught her?' he said, staring down at Gracie. 'Who has caught her?'

'The Captain,' Gracie said, looking nervously about. 'They ambushed Naomi. She was helping a girl and then they took her.'

Valen reached out and grabbed Gracie by the collar. He pulled her into his shop and slammed the door closed. 'Come to my office and sit on the couch. I will make some tea.'

'We need to get her,' Gracie said, wringing her hands. 'There is no time for tea.'

'Go and sit on the couch, young lady,' Valen said, pointing to his office. 'We cannot just run out into the early morning darkness. I need more information.'

Gracie turned on her heels and marched into the office. She dropped onto the couch and folded her arms.

Valen slammed two mugs onto the kitchen counter. 'Tell me what happened.'

'Naomi was trying to rescue some girls from Donte,' Gracie said. 'But it was a trap. The guards were waiting for her. We need to get her.'

The office chair groaned as Valen sat on it. He passed a mug of tea to Gracie. 'What are the sewer rats doing about it?'

Gracie balanced the mug on the armrest. 'Nothing. Naomi said they should stay hidden if anything like this happens.'

Valen frowned. 'They won't do anything?'

'What can they do?' Gracie said, her voice rising. 'The sewer rats shouldn't even exist.'

With a grumble, Valen sat back in his chair. He placed the mug on his desk. 'I don't know what I can do, Gracie.'

Gracie suddenly got up. The mug crashed to the ground. 'How can you just sit there? They are going to kill her.'

'Whoa, calm down,' Valen said, holding out his hands. 'Who said anything about killing her?'

'I heard it from some people on the way here,' Gracie said. 'They will parade her in the square before they pass sentence. A man said he thinks they will put her to death.'

From deep in his barrel chest, a low growl rose out of Valen's mouth. He stood and walked through the kitchen and up the stairs.

'Where are you going?' Gracie said.

'Wait there,' Valen shouted down the stairs. 'I am getting some stuff and then we are going to the square.'

'Hurry please,' Gracie said.

Valen rummaged around in his wardrobe until he found his old multicoloured jersey. He threw it over his worn shirt and pulled the sleeves up halfway to his elbows. The cloak stand rattled as he ripped his cloak off it. In the corner of his room sat a wicked-looking club. He reached for it, then changed his mind. He double-stepped down the stairs and into the office.

'They are still going to know it's you,' Gracie said, a smirk breaking her worried face. 'You can't hide in a cloak.'

'It makes me feel better,' Valen said. 'Come on, let's get moving.'

The front doorbell tinkled. Gracie pulled the hood of her cloak over her head. She reached into her hood and clicked the mask over her mouth. The black mask blended into her skin and covered most of her face. The only thing Valen could see were her angry, dark-brown eyes. A light, orange glow filled the sky as the sun in the east broke the horizon.

'You know the drill,' Valen said. 'Any trouble and you must get yourself into the alleys, OK?'

Gracie said nothing, but she gave him a nod.

They hurried north through the winding roads until up ahead, the east–west road came into view.

'Hey, outsider,' a man shouted from a shop door. 'I hear they have caught your lover. Going to sentence her to death, we have heard.'

'You are talking crazy, sir,' Valen said, shaking his head at the man. 'Why would they put a girl to death?'

The man lifted his eyes to the sky. 'Poor outsider. He still hasn't understood how Fairacre works. She is a woman and a sewer rat. They will hang her to make an example of her.'

Valen's mouth fell open. 'Hang? What do you mean, hang?'

'By the neck,' the man said, twisting his neck to one side. 'It will be quick. Best you hurry and pay your respects, outsider.'

Gracie grabbed Valen by the hand. 'We need to move or we will be too late.'

Valen blinked, then shook his head. 'I don't understand what is happening.'

They turned left onto the east–west road and made for the town square. The buildings along the road lay deserted as all the women workers lined the shop walls. They strained their necks to get a view of the town square in the far-off distance.

'They will hang her,' a woman whispered as Valen and Gracie walked past.

'Hanged by the neck with everyone watching,' another said.

'All she has done is try to help the orphans,' a girl said, leaning on her broom.

Valen increased his stride. Gracie hopped along to keep up with the big man. Up ahead, the jeering of men broke through the morning stillness. As they got closer, Valen slowed and bit his bottom lip at Naomi, who stood at the top of the steps. Her cut lip shimmered. Blood dripped down over her chin. Both eyes, a deep purple, peered out of closing slits.

'What have they done to you?' Valen said under his breath. 'How dare these animals!'

A growl escaped Gracie's lips. Valen pulled her close to him as he worked his way through the crowd.

'We have caught the leader of the sewer rats,' the Captain shouted. 'My officers and I placed a trap. She walked straight into it.'

A whistle sounded from a rooftop. Valen swung his head and glimpsed a masked face peering over the roof's gutter. He looked back at Naomi and saw the small shake of the head she gave back to the sewer rats.

'She is telling them to stay away,' Gracie whispered. 'She doesn't want anyone else getting caught.'

28

Valen knelt and placed his hands on Gracie's shoulders. 'You need to listen to me.'

'I am not going anywhere,' Gracie said defiantly. 'I want to help.'

A ghost of a smile crept across Valen's face as he looked at the strong young girl. 'You need to be with the sewer rats. You can help a lot more by being with them. If you stay with me, it might get ugly and you will end up standing next to Naomi.'

Gracie bit her bottom lip, then threw her arms around Valen's neck. 'Please save her.'

'I will try my best,' Valen said. 'Now go. Get to your sisters.'

With a nod, Gracie disappeared into the crowd. Valen stood and faced the opposite direction to where Naomi stood. After a few moments, he glimpsed the hooded figure of Gracie disappear down an alley. He cast his eyes to the roof and waited until she appeared next to her sewer-rat sisters.

'Here goes nothing,' Valen said, turning around.

'It will be up to Mr Hargreaves to sentence this rat,' the Captain spat. 'I have given my recommendation of hanging by the neck.'

The crowd cheered.

'What is going on?' Valen thundered, as he barged towards the town hall steps. 'Why have you hurt this woman?'

The entire square fell into a deathly silence. All at once, they spun around and stared at him.

'Do you not know who this rat is, eh, outsider?' a man spat on the ground. 'This menace, this woman, has been terrorising the town for over a year. We must put her away for good. Mustn't we, eh, outsider?'

'She is my friend,' Valen said. 'She helps young girls when they haven't got a place to stay.'

'Did you just say that this woman is your friend, eh, outsider?' the man said. 'We all knew there was something

29

wrong with you. Maybe you should join her up there, eh, outsider?'

Valen took a step back as the crowd moved towards him. 'You animals. How dare you hurt a woman so?'

'She is a thief, eh, outsider,' the man snarled. 'Her and her gang of sewer rats raid the markets and the fields and take our food and supplies.'

'She is just feeding a few homeless girls,' Valen said, holding his hands up. 'Nobody should have to starve.'

The town's men surrounded him, leaving him standing alone in a circle.

'He is a traitor,' another man hissed. 'We have always known he is trouble.'

'I don't want any trouble,' Valen said. 'Please, just give me the girl and I will leave.'

The man snarled. 'Just give him the girl, he says. He will leave us alone, he says. I think you have misjudged this situation, eh, outsider? You are the one in trouble now.'

'I said I don't want any trouble,' Valen repeated, his voice lowering into a snarl.

'Get him!' the man shouted, pointing at Valen.

Valen swung a big boot and connected with the man's chest. As the man flew into the crowd, he knocked over a couple of other men. The men roared and rushed at Valen. With a swing of his enormous fist, he connected with a few men who crumpled in a heap on the ground. More men joined until they rushed at him from every direction. Eventually, with the sheer weight and force of the men, Valen couldn't swing his arms and legs any longer. He raised his hands to protect himself. A blast of pain coursed through his legs as something struck him on the back of his left knee. His left leg collapsed. He fell onto a knee. Another crack sounded across the square as something else struck him across his back. His other leg collapsed. He dropped to his other knee. 'I don't want any trouble,' he said, trying to get back onto his feet. 'Leave the girl alone and leave me alone.'

'Take him down!' a man shouted.

More men rushed at Valen and piled on top of him. Boots, fists and knees caught him in the back and face. Valen pulled his knees up to his chest and pulled his arms over his head. The blows continued to strike every exposed part of his body. Coppery blood filled his mouth. Darkness came and went as occasionally a fist got through his defences and hit him on the side of the head.

'Stop!' a voice shouted.

The blows stopped.

'Move, please. Get out of my way,' the voice said.

'Yes, Mr Hargreaves,' a man said.

'What is going on here?' Mr Hargreaves said. 'We have enough trouble with these sewer rats without us turning on each other.'

'He wanted to save the girl, eh,' the man said, wiping blood from the corner of his mouth. 'He is in favour of letting her go.'

'We must hang her, Mr Hargreaves,' another man shouted.

'Keep quiet,' Mr Hargreaves thundered. 'Even if she is to be hanged, we do not treat our own like this.'

'He is an outsider, eh,' the man spat. 'Just another dog coming into our town and taking our jobs and our women.'

'Be quiet,' Mr Hargreaves said. 'You have no problem having outsiders working your fields, do you?'

'What do we do with him, eh, sir? What do we do with him?' the man said, ignoring Mr Hargreaves's comment.

'Clear him out of the square,' Mr Hargreaves said. 'And if I hear you have harmed this man further, I will throw you into jail myself.'

Rough hands grabbed Valen. He felt the roughness of the cobblestones on his back as they dragged him. Pain shot through his eyes as the back of his head cracked against a kerb. The men lifted Valen to a sitting position and propped him up against one of the house walls.

'Disgusting outsider,' a man said, slapping Valen through the face.

Valen opened a swollen eye and watched Mr Hargreaves climb the steps to the town hall. Naomi stood with her head bowed. Another droplet of blood fell from her chin, splashing onto the cobblestone ground.

'Hang her,' a man shouted.

Valen's forehead crinkled in surprise as he watched Mr Hargreaves lean in and whisper something into Naomi's ear.

'Stone her,' another man shouted. 'Stone this sewer-rat filth.'

Mr Hargreaves held up a hand. 'There will be no hanging or stoning today.'

The crowd grew silent.

'She is a thief,' a man said. 'Her thieving sewer rats have ruined my life. We demand you hang her.'

'She has hardly ruined your life,' Mr Hargreaves said, looking down at the man and shaking his head. 'You have earned enough to send your daughters to the finishing schools on the cliffs. So last time I checked, you were doing just fine, sir.'

The man spat on the ground. 'Thieving rags, the lot of 'em.'

'We will take the leader of the sewer rats to the City of Lynn,' Mr Hargreaves said. 'The Queen herself has requested an audience. We will hold her in the jails until the Queen's transport arrives.'

'Unacceptable,' a man shouted. 'We deserve justice. Why does the Queen want to see her?'

'I am sure the Queen will punish her for her actions,' Mr Hargreaves said. 'It is the Queen's rules she has broken. Guards, take her to the jails and place a guard next to her cell. If anyone tries to harm her, they will answer to me.'

'Unbelievable,' a man muttered as he walked out of the square and past Valen.

'Look at this dog,' another man said, kicking Valen in the legs.

'He is one of them,' a man said.

Valen opened his eye, then slammed it shut as the bottom of a man's boot crashed into his face.

Valen cracked open an eye. He brought a hand up to his face and winced as his finger touched a swollen lump. With a lick of his dry lips, he groaned at the sharp stabs of pain. The alley that he sat in lay dark and quiet. The smells of discarded, rotting food and stagnant water made him scrunch up his nose. In the west, the sun had already set.

'Outsider dog,' a man shouted into the alley.

Valen placed a hand on the wall behind him and pushed himself to his feet. He ran his hands over his body, feeling for broken bones. A sigh of relief escaped him as he found that everything was intact. His head, though, throbbed painfully with every breath. The ground swayed under his feet as he took his first step forward.

'Home,' Valen said, the taste of blood flooding his mouth.

He took a step and stumbled. A hand reached out of the darkness and grabbed hold of his elbow.

'Who is there?' Valen said, trying to pull his arm away.

'I will not hurt you,' a woman said.

'Who are you?' Valen said, scrunching up his eyes and looking into the darkness. 'Why are you hiding?'

'My name is Chloe and I will stay right where I am,' Chloe said.

'Valen,' Gracie said, jumping down from the rooftop.

'Stay right there, Gracie,' Chloe said sternly.

'Gracie? Are you OK?' Valen said, taking a step forward. 'Where are you?'

'Gracie is just fine,' Chloe said. 'You, on the other hand, look terrible.'

Valen ran his hand over his blood-caked face and grimaced. 'I need to get home.'

'We will lead you there,' Chloe said.

Hands grabbed Valen's elbows. He blinked to get a glimpse of the figures that led him through the alleys. Suddenly, someone hissed. Valen buckled down to his knees as hands shoved him to the ground.

'What is going on?' he said.

'Quiet,' Chloe said. 'Guards are coming.'

Valen heard the march of boots turn towards them.

'What do we do, boss?' a woman said.

'Stay hidden,' Chloe said. 'They cannot see us in here.'

The guards stopped. 'Have we checked all these alleys?' one said.

'Yes, sir,' another replied in a bored tone.

'Move towards the square then,' the other guard said.

The march of boots moved up the street.

'Let's go,' Chloe said.

Valen groaned as hands lifted him to his feet. As they broke out of the alley, he stumbled, but he remained standing as the hands pushed him upright.

'We aren't far now, Valen,' Gracie said, catching up and walking next to him.

Valen blinked at the locs that bounced in front of him. The tall, black girl strode towards the other side of the street and into another alley.

'Oh no,' Gracie said, seeing Valen's face for the first time. 'What have they done to you?'

'Come on, Gracie,' Chloe said over her shoulder. 'We can sort him out when we get home.'

Gracie grabbed one of Valen's hands and squeezed. 'Are you OK?'

Valen grinned, then grimaced. 'I will be better when we get home—'

'And have a cup of tea?' Gracie said, finishing his sentence.

'Yes, and have a cup of tea,' Valen said, trying not to grin.

They entered the alley across the street. Chloe slowed and waited for them to catch up.

Valen watched three girls overtake Chloe and continue through the alleys. 'Are you the sewer rats?' he said.

'You know we are the sewer rats,' Chloe said. 'This is my team.'

'What have they done with Naomi?' Valen said.

'We don't know,' Chloe said, turning down another alley. 'She is being held in the jails and we cannot get anyone to her.'

'I tried to get them to free her,' Valen said.

'I understand,' Chloe said. 'But I think you may have done more damage than good.'

Valen bowed his head. 'I didn't figure they hated her so much.'

'We are all hated,' Chloe said. 'Come, keep walking. We need to get you home.'

Valen concentrated on keeping up with the sewer rats. With the blood now pumping through his body properly, he could feel all the painful bumps and bruises the men had given him. He could, however, move more easily. Chloe turned into the winding street that led to Valen's shop.

'How do you know which way to go?' Valen said.

Chloe flashed a smile over her shoulder. 'Do you think we would let one of our young ones come and see someone without them being protected?'

'How silly of me,' Valen said. 'I didn't know you had brought your own protection detail, Gracie.'

'You are famous, Valen,' Gracie said, her voice cracking with concern.

Valen pulled Gracie closer to him. 'It's OK, lass. I am banged up, but I am OK.'

'Lass?' Chloe said over her shoulder. 'What does that mean?'

'It means girl,' Gracie said.

'Ahh,' Chloe said. 'Look, we are here at your secret, not-so-secret shop.'

'Home sweet home, Valen,' Gracie said.

Chloe opened the shop door. The bell tinkled through the night. 'Wait here,' she said.

'Why?' Valen said, taking a step forward.

'Because I said so,' Chloe said, placing a hand on his chest.

Valen grunted.

'Please listen to Chloe,' Gracie said. 'She knows what she is doing, Valen.'

Valen watched two girls disappear into his shop. 'Like I need to be protected,' he muttered to himself. 'Protected by girls.'

'You are doing a fine job of looking after yourself, aren't you?' Chloe said. 'They are just checking your place because you are a marked man.'

After a few minutes, a girl appeared at the front door. 'It's quiet, miss.'

'In you go,' Chloe said. 'Get yourself cleaned up.'

Valen walked into his shop and up the stairs to his room. He stripped off his blood-caked clothes and walked into the shower room. He waited for cold water to fall from the tank that sat on top of the house. With the muscle in his jaw twitching, he dived under the water. A long groan escaped his lips as the water touched the cuts and grazes. A few minutes later, he climbed out of the shower room, dressed, and made his way down to his office. With a rattle of his lips, Valen lowered himself into his office chair.

'How are you feeling?' Gracie said.

'I am very sore, but they didn't break any bones,' Valen said.

'It was a very brave thing you did out there,' Chloe said from the kitchen.

'Brave, or stupid?' Valen said.

Chloe chuckled. 'I think you will find they are much of the same thing most of the time.'

'I don't understand it,' Valen said. 'Why would they want to hang Naomi? I know the rules in this town are strict and do not favour women, but to hang someone? I don't understand.'

Chloe walked into the office and placed a mug of tea on the desk for Valen. She lowered herself onto the couch and draped a long black leg over the armrest. She handed another mug of tea to Gracie.

'You have no clue, do you?' Chloe said.

'Obviously not,' Valen said, taking a sip of tea. 'Dr Viktor is a man from the old ways and always said that women should know their place. But never was it mentioned that a hanging would be involved.'

Chloe's leg bounced up and down on the armrest. 'Women are owned in this town, Valen. You know that because everyone keeps telling you to buy a wife. All the women who the men don't buy end up discarded. They either work for a man like Donte, who treats his girls like slaves, or they escape and become part of the sewer rats.'

'Next you will tell me you live in the sewers,' Valen said with a snort.

Chloe raised an eyebrow.

'No you don't,' Valen said.

Chloe lifted her other eyebrow.

'You live in the sewers? The actual sewers?'

'We do,' Chloe said, blowing on her tea. 'There are a lot of us down there.'

Valen whistled, then winced as his lips cracked again. He looked at Gracie. 'You never told me it was the actual sewers. I just thought it was something you called yourself and the place that you live.'

Gracie glanced at Chloe. 'It is a rule. I am not allowed to show anyone where we live.'

'And she didn't break the rule, so I am very proud of her,' Chloe said, ruffling her hair.

'Are you two related?' Valen said.

Chloe grinned. 'No. But our parents both come from the west.'

Valen moved in his chair and let out a groan.

'Are you sure they didn't break anything?' Chloe said.

'Just my pride,' Valen said.

'You look a right mess,' Chloe said.

'Bruises and cuts,' Valen said. 'My big fear is my eyes and hands. I cannot do my work if they don't work.'

'I would say that is the case for most people,' Chloe said.

'Aye, lass, but I need my hands to do delicate work, not smash-things-up type work.'

Chloe crinkled her forehead at the little beasts that sat on the shelves above Valen's desk. 'You made those small things?'

Valen looked up at the shelves, then looked back at Chloe. 'You look surprised?'

'I am,' Chloe said. 'You deal in arts and crafts, but I didn't know you made them, too. What of the one on your desk?'

'That's Ssia the ssnake,' Gracie said. 'And the spider is Henry and the bumblebee is Jay. I want to build beasts one day as well.'

Chloe smiled at Gracie. 'I thought you wanted to be a warrior.'

'I can be both,' Gracie said, raising her chin.

'Yes, you can,' Chloe said, smiling at her. She turned to Valen. 'Can I take a look at them?'

'Aye, lass,' Valen said, reaching up and picking the boxed bumblebee from the shelf. 'Be careful with him now.'

Chloe took the box and brought it close to her face. 'So detailed,' she said. 'How did you fold metal that fine?'

Valen picked up a toolkit from the other side of his desk and rolled it out onto his lap. 'I use these tools given to me by Dr Viktor,' he said, running his fingers over the tiny tools.

'I don't see how those tools can bend metal this fine,' Chloe said, raising an eyebrow.

Valen shrugged. 'Well, they work for me.'

Chloe froze.

'What is it, lass?' Valen said, sitting forward and catching his tools before they slid off his lap.

'I thought I saw the bee move,' Chloe said, eyeing the small bumblebee.

With deft hands, Valen rolled up the tool belt and placed it on the desk. He gently took the box from Chloe and placed it on the shelf.

'I think it is time we get going,' Chloe said, lifting her leg off the armrest.

'What is going to happen to Naomi?' Valen said.

'We will get Naomi back,' Chloe said, sitting forward. 'Please don't get involved. You will just cause more trouble.'

'Mr Hargreaves will listen to me,' Valen said. 'I can speak to him and find out what is going on.'

Chloe stood. 'You can speak to him, but it will do no good. Mr Hargreaves is bound by the laws of Fairacre. He will do what is required of him.'

Valen took a deep breath. 'Isn't there anything I can do?'

The couch crunched as Chloe sat back in it. She threw her leg over the armrest and stared unblinkingly at Valen. 'Can I trust you to not mess things up?'

'If you tell me what to do?' Valen said.

'Fighting in the middle of the square is what you shouldn't be doing,' Chloe said, smirking. 'You can help by getting us information.'

'What type of information?' Valen said, sitting forward with a grimace.

'We need to know where Naomi is and what it looks like down in the jails. We can get into the jails through the sewers, but we don't know what the layout is and who will be down there with her.'

Valen rubbed his chin. 'I think I may have a way to help.'

'Oh really?' Chloe said, raising both her eyebrows. 'Tell me how you are going to help when everyone in Fairacre knows who you are and that you are friends with Naomi?'

Valen let out a sigh. 'I can get the information out of Hargreaves, somehow.'

'If that is something you can do, then do it,' Chloe said, sitting forward. 'You can also continue to help like you have always helped. By supplying us with some food and something to keep the children distracted. They are going to need it now more than ever.'

The office chair creaked as Valen sat back into it. He narrowed his eyes as his face slowly turned to icy stone anger. With an almighty bang, he slammed his hand down on his desk.

Gracie jumped. Chloe's leg stopped bouncing.

'Sorry,' Valen grumbled. 'I am furious at what they are doing. It is disgusting, ignorant behaviour.'

'You really care for Naomi, don't you?' Chloe said.

'Naomi and Valen sitting in a tree,' Gracie said.

'Stop it,' Valen said, wagging a finger at Gracie. 'I care for Naomi, but not in that way.'

'What do you mean, not in that way?' Chloe said, the corners of her mouth turning up.

'You know what I mean,' Valen said, rolling his bloodshot eyes. 'I care for her, but not how Gracie thinks.'

Gracie crossed her arms and looked up at the ceiling. 'Boring.'

Chloe chuckled as she stood. 'It is time for me to go. Get some rest, Valen.'

Valen stood and followed Chloe, Gracie and the other girls to the front door of his shop. 'I will think of a way to get the information you need.'

'OK,' Chloe said. 'But be careful.'

'Are you sure you are going to be OK?' Gracie said, looking at Valen with concern.

'I will be just fine, lass,' Valen said.

Chloe reached up and held the doorbell. 'You should remove this bell for a while. If we are to come and go, we don't want your neighbours hearing.'

Valen nodded as he watched the sewer rats dart across the road and into the alley.

CHAPTER 3
THEY ARE ALIVE

The next morning, Valen woke up and immediately let out a long groan. The back of his head throbbed. Round bruises on his body glared a dark blue and purple. Shallow cuts had opened up during the night, leaving small specks of blood trailing across his bed sheets. He swung his feet onto the floor and took in a sharp breath to counter the pain that ran up his legs. The floorboards creaked as he stumbled over to the bathroom. In the bathroom, he looked into the mirror and shook his head at the ghastly sight looking back at him.

'Is everything OK?'

Valen's head cracked against the bathroom door as he turned in fright. 'What are you doing here?' he shouted, rubbing the side of his head.

'Chloe said I need to keep an eye on you,' the woman said.

'I don't need a babysitter,' Valen said. 'And I certainly don't need anyone in my room or watching me shower.'

The woman raised an eyebrow.

'Suit yourself then,' Valen said, turning around and stripping off his shirt.

'I will wait for you in your office,' the woman said, leaving.

Valen closed the bathroom door and turned the lever on the shower. The jarring cold water slammed into his body, making him gasp. He took his time washing off the patches of caked-on blood. After towelling himself dry and dressing, he made his way down to the kitchen. 'So why has Chloe sent me a babysitter?' he said, while grabbing two mugs from the cupboard.

'Who are you speaking to, outsider?' a man said.

Valen peered into his store, then let out a growl. 'What are you doing in my shop, Dec?'

'I have it under good authority that you have been hiding sewer rats in your shop,' Dec said, folding his arms. 'Tell me the truth, outsider.'

Valen stopped making his tea and walked down to his office door. He leant against the door frame and reached for his club.

'A young girl who dresses like a boy,' Jon said, stepping out from behind the shelves.

Valen counted more men lingering outside his shop. He let go of the club and folded his arms.

'You didn't think we knew, outsider?' Dec said. 'Of course we knew. Everyone knows you have been hiding those filthy rats in your shop.'

'I don't know what you are talking about,' Valen said, rubbing his cut chin. 'I would appreciate it if you either bought something or left my shop.'

Dec walked around the counter and up the middle aisle. He stopped at a big box that sat on the middle shelf. 'What do we have in here? This box looks very important, doesn't it, Jon?'

'Very important, Dec,' Jon said, as he rested both elbows on the shop counter. 'I wonder what's inside it?'

The box slipped off the shelf and crashed to the floor. Colouring-in pencils and colouring books spilled across the floor.

'Seems like toys for children, outsider,' Dec said. 'Have you been sending these things to the sewer rats? Have you been supplying those filthy rats?'

Valen walked up the aisle and stopped inches from Dec's face. 'Do that again and I will make you pay for it.'

Dec lifted his chin and roared with laughter. Jon, hearing Dec's laugh, raised his head and joined in.

'Get out of my shop,' Valen hissed.

'Or what?' Jon said. 'What are you going to do, outsider?'

'I am speaking to Mr Hargreaves today,' Valen said. 'What do you think he will say about your brief visit?'

The guards stared at Valen with unblinking eyes. Dec stood on his toes until his eyes were at the same height as Valen's. 'You tell Hargreaves anything about this visit and we will throw your little friend into prison.'

Valen curled a lip. 'If you hurt him in any way, I will hunt you all down.'

'You mean her,' Jon said. 'Yes, outsider. We are not stupid. We know she is a girl.'

Dec laughed. 'Look at the outsider's face turn all red, Jon.'

Valen took a step forward and bumped Dec with his chest. 'I suggest you get out of here now,' he said, his eyes narrowing.

'Let's go, Dec,' Jon said, smirking. 'We need to hunt down some more sewer rats.'

Dec walked backwards down the aisle. Halfway down, he kicked another box off its shelf. The sound of glass shattering vibrated through the shop.

'Get out,' Valen said, taking a step and pointing at the front door.

Jon opened the door and held it until Dec stepped out. 'Remember, outsider. If you tell anyone about this visit, we will make sure the ones you care about get seriously hurt.'

'Get out!' Valen shouted.

The front door slammed shut, but no doorbell sound filled the store. Valen walked around the counter and spotted the bell in the room's corner.

'Chloe wanted you to remove that,' the woman said from behind him.

Valen jumped. 'Do you have to sneak up on me like that?'

The girl raised her eyebrows again.

'If I had kept this bell fitted, I would have heard them coming,' Valen said. 'I am going to keep it on the door.'

The woman shrugged. 'Your funeral.'

'What is your name?' Valen said.

'Alexa,' the woman said. 'I am part of Chloe's team.'

Valen picked up a broom and started cleaning his shop. 'A lot of help you were with that lot. All you did was hide.'

Alexa smiled. 'I am not here to save you from them. I am here to stop you from causing trouble for Naomi.'

'I am not going anywhere,' Valen said.

Alexa stepped out of the way of Valen's broom. A few minutes later, Valen walked back into the kitchen and carried on making tea for himself and Alexa. With the tea ready, he walked back into his office and stopped halfway to his desk. 'Hello, Gracie,' he said.

'Where is my tea?' Gracie said, smiling sweetly.

Valen handed Alexa her tea and handed Gracie his own. He walked back into the kitchen and made another cup.

'What are you doing today?' Gracie said.

'Once I finish my beast, I will go and speak to Mr Hargreaves,' Valen said. 'I am going to get to the bottom of Naomi's arrest.'

'I am going to come with you,' Gracie said.

Valen walked back into the office and lowered himself into his chair. 'No, you are not. There is no way you are going to the town hall.'

Gracie's mouth hung open. 'Why not?'

'Because Dec and Jon will hurt you if they see us together,' Valen said.

'But,' Gracie said, her shoulders slumping.

'Hush, Gracie,' Alexa said, with a shake of her head. 'Valen is right. The guards know you are a girl and part of the sewer rats. You can come into the shop, but you cannot go out there with Valen.'

Gracie placed her mug on the armrest and folded her arms. 'This is so unfair.'

'What is unfair?' Chloe said from the office doorway.

'Can you people stop sneaking into my shop?' Valen hissed with a shake of his head. 'I feel like my place is haunted.'

'I told you to get rid of this,' Chloe said, wagging the doorbell at Valen.

'Give me that,' Valen said, trying to snatch the bell from Chloe. 'Stop messing with my stuff.'

Chloe gave Valen a smile. 'Keep the doorbell off the door.'

Valen fell back into his office chair. 'Yes, ma'am.'

'Any news about Naomi, boss?' Alexa said.

'Not much, other than she is being held in the prison,' Chloe said, finding a space on the couch. 'They don't treat people well down there, though, so we need to get her out as quickly as possible.'

'I am going to speak to Hargreaves,' Valen said, pushing his chair back and getting to his feet. 'I trust I can leave my shop in your capable hands?'

'Please don't let us find you in another alley,' Chloe said.

'There aren't enough guards to take me down this time,' Valen said, flexing his massive shoulders. 'You might stumble onto some of them in the alley, though. That's if they get in my way.'

Chloe chuckled. 'OK, big man. We will wait for you here.'

'I want to go with,' Gracie said.

'No,' Valen, Chloe and Alexa said in unison.

Gracie looked up at the ceiling. 'Boring!'

Valen left his shop and made his way towards the city centre. As he walked through the streets, the town's men either ignored him or sneered at him. The women pointed and whispered. Valen ignored both and kept his gaze front and centre. He turned left onto the east–west road and walked towards the city square.

'Outsider, dog,' a man said as they walked past each other. 'I see you are still alive. What a pity.'

Valen kept his eyes firmly straight ahead. Once he reached the square, he walked to the northern side and walked up the steps to the doors of the town hall.

'What do you want?' the guard at the door said.

'I wish to see Mr Hargreaves. He knows who I am.'

'He is not taking any guests today,' the guard said, curling his lip. 'Especially a sewer-rat-loving dog. Come back never. You understand, outsider?'

'I will see him today,' Valen said, placing his hand on the door.

The guard reached for his sword. 'Mr Hargreaves is not seeing anyone at the moment. Which part of that sentence did you not understand?'

'I have had enough of this,' Valen said. 'Move aside or I will move you aside.'

Just as the guard's sword reached halfway out of its sheath, Valen snapped the guard's head back with a swift punch to the underside of his chin. Before the guard hit the ground, Valen caught him and dragged him through the town hall doors. At the first corner Valen could find, he propped the guard up against the wall.

'Who goes there?' a man shouted.

'Hargreaves,' Valen thundered. 'Where are you?'

'What the hell are you doing here?' Mr Hargreaves shouted. 'Do you know how dangerous this is, Valen? Get out of here, you silly fool.'

Valen made his way to the back of the town hall, where he shoved open a set of double doors. A corridor lined with offices led to Mr Hargreaves's office. The mayor's office door lay open.

'Come in,' Mr Hargreaves said, after Valen had already walked through the door.

'What is going on, Hargreaves?' Valen said, spreading his legs and folding his arms. 'You are locking up young women now. Beating them so they bleed. What kind of man are you?'

'She is the leader of the sewer rats,' Hargreaves said as he stood and walked around his desk. 'It was silly of her to get caught in the first place.'

'You have not answered my question,' Valen said. 'What type of man beats a woman? Tell me, Hargreaves.'

'It wasn't me, Valen,' Mr Hargreaves said, spreading his arms. 'According to the Captain, she wouldn't come quietly and put up a fight. She put three guards in hospital.'

'Good! Now you need to let her go,' Valen said, using his height to lean over Mr Hargreaves. 'You know this isn't right. Get her out of that jail.'

Mr Hargreaves held up his hands. 'There is nothing I can do. The Queen has requested we send her to the City of Lynn. What am I supposed to do? Defy the Queen?'

Valen backed Mr Hargreaves towards the oak desk. He leant in so their noses nearly touched. 'This is disgusting, Hargreaves. You are disgusting. The way you treat our women in this town is horrific. It makes me sick.'

'What do you expect me to do?' Mr Hargreaves said, leaning back over his desk. 'The City of Lynn sets the laws and we follow them. It is punishable by death if we disobey.'

Valen stepped back, kicked a chair into place, then lowered himself into it. 'It's disgusting,' he snarled.

'You are playing with fire consorting with the sewer rats,' Mr Hargreaves said as he walked around his desk and sat. 'I cannot protect you if the Captain catches you with them.'

'I am very close to having a run-in with your captain,' Valen said. 'And that will turn ugly. I won't let anybody get the better of me again like they did in the square.'

'That is another terrible idea,' Mr Hargreaves said, picking up a pen and tapping it on the desk. 'The Captain is from the City of Lynn and will report back to the Queen.'

'I couldn't care less who he reports back to,' Valen said. 'Now, how do I get Naomi out of that jail, Hargreaves?'

Mr Hargreaves dropped his pen. 'You don't, Valen. The Queen's Guard will be here in a few days and she is being taken to the City.'

Valen stared at Mr Hargreaves. A minute later, he said. 'Is she being looked after? Down in that jail. Is she being looked after, Hargreaves?'

'She is being fed and left alone, if that is what you mean?' Mr Hargreaves said.

'What about her injuries?' Valen said.

Mr Hargreaves shrugged. 'Nothing I can do about that. Those are her own fault.'

Valen shook his head. 'You can do better than that. How many guards have you got down there?'

'Are you fishing for information, Valen?' Mr Hargreaves said. 'There are six guards down there at all times, so don't get any bright ideas.'

Valen rubbed the stubble on his chin.

'Not even you could take on six guards, Valen,' Mr Hargreaves said. 'And if you take them on, you know I will have to lock you up.'

'What are they going to do with her in the City?' Valen said.

'I have no idea,' Mr Hargreaves said.

'Is there anything you do know?' Valen said, raising both hands and shrugging his shoulders.

An almighty bang of a slamming door rang through the town hall.

'That's the Captain,' Mr Hargreaves said. 'You need to get out of here.'

Valen pulled himself to his feet and walked into the corridor. He tried each office door until he found one unlocked. Closing the door quietly behind him, he crouched down underneath the window. A few moments later, the Captain walked down the corridor, past his window, and into Mr Hargreaves's office.

'What is it, Captain?' Mr Hargreaves said.

'Have you seen the guard at the front door?' the Captain said.

'What are you talking about?' Mr Hargreaves said.

'The guard at the front of the town hall? Oh, forget about it,' the Captain said. 'I will deal with him later.'

'How can I help you?' Mr Hargreaves said.

'We have been tracking the sewer rats and I think we may have found a way to track them into their home.'

'Hold off on that for a minute, Captain,' Mr Hargreaves said. 'We have bigger things to tackle. How is the leader doing?'

'They beat her up but she will survive unfortunately. We had to swap out some guards as they were conspiring to kill her.'

'Keep her alive, Captain. That is your number one priority. We can discuss the sewer rats once the Queen has taken their leader.'

'We need to go now while they don't have a leader,' the Captain said. 'I propose I go down there and eliminate all of them.'

'Please, Captain, close the door and take a seat,' Mr Hargreaves said.

The door of Mr Hargreaves's office banged shut. Valen pressed his ear against the wall and listened. All he could hear were murmurs. With a frustrated sigh, he crept out of the office and through the double doors into the town hall. He jogged to the corner where he had left the guard. The guard still sat snoring, propped up against the wall. Valen swung open the door and walked into the streaming sunlight. He placed his hand on his brow to block the sun. The square lay empty. As he walked down the steps, he heard a tweet from the rooftop. He scanned each roof until he found movement. Across the square, he saw a lone figure lying on the roof. Gracie lifted her hand and waved at Valen.

Valen shook his head as he waved Gracie away.

Gracie disappeared then seconds later reappeared on another corner of the roof.

Another tweet and another wave. With another shake of his head, Valen walked across the town hall square and made his way back to his shop.

The shop door opened but there was no tinkling bell. Valen marched around the counter, down the shop aisle, and into his office. He stopped and listened. 'I know you are all here. Stop hiding, sewer-rat ghosts.'

'Good to see you are becoming more aware,' Chloe said, stepping out of the shadows.

'The Captain says he can track you to the sewers,' Valen said, ignoring Chloe's comment.

Chloe stopped dead. 'What did you say?'

'I heard the Captain speak to Mr Hargreaves,' Valen said. 'He said they have a way to get to your home.'

'Did he say when this was going to happen?' Alexa said from behind Valen.

Valen jumped. 'Sneaky sewer rats,' he muttered. 'Mr Hargreaves told the Captain to wait until they transported Naomi to the City of Lynn.'

'In a couple of days,' Chloe said. 'We need to get the sewer rats moved.'

'We need to get Naomi back,' Gracie said. 'She will know what to do.'

Valen looked at Gracie, then at the front door, then back at Gracie. 'How did you get in here?'

Gracie frowned. 'There are a lot of ways into your shop, Valen.'

The office chair groaned as Valen sank into it. 'How are we going to get Naomi back?'

'What else did you find out?' Chloe said.

'There are six guards looking after Naomi. Mr Hargreaves warned me they are looking out for any rescue attempt from me.'

'Make that eight then,' Alexa said. 'Mr Hargreaves would not have told the truth. And if they are looking out for you, it means they will be looking out for the sewer rats.'

'Too many for us to make a surprise attack through the sewers,' Chloe said, sitting on the couch and draping her leg over the arm rest.

'We need to bring some of the guards to the surface,' Alexa said.

Quiet descended on the office as each of them disappeared into their own thoughts.

'Why don't the sewer rats distract them?' Gracie said, suddenly. 'We could lead them down into the sewers, then away from our home.'

'Wouldn't guarantee that all guards would leave the jail,' Alexa said. 'Also, it's a bit risky as the guards might stumble into our home.'

Valen looked at Chloe, then Alexa, then Gracie. He leant back in his chair and let out a long sigh.

'What is up with you?' Chloe said, raising both eyebrows.

With a shake of his head, Valen dropped his head into his hands and mumbled something.

'What?' Gracie said, her voice rising. 'What is wrong with you?'

Valen sat back in his chair and rocked backwards and forwards. 'I promised I would never ever do this again.'

'Promised what?' Gracie said. 'You are talking in riddles, Valen. You know that is my job, not yours.'

'I may have a way to distract the guards,' Valen said. 'But to do so, I have to break a promise I made to myself a long time ago.'

Chloe's leg stopped bouncing. 'I don't want you to do anything you don't want to do, but there is a lot at stake here, Valen. Naomi needs our help, and the sewer rats are in trouble.'

Valen closed his eyes, leant back, and took in a long, deep breath, which he released in a wave of lip rattling.

'So dramatic,' Gracie said, lifting her eyes towards the ceiling. 'You are worse than Dec and Jon.'

The office chair squeaked as Valen spun to face his desk. He plucked the boxes of the spider and the bumblebee from the top shelf and put them on the desk. He opened the boxes and got out the two beasts, placing them on the surface in front of him. With his eyes closed, he murmured the words Dr Viktor had taught him.

'What are you doing?' Gracie said as she pushed herself off the couch and stood next to him. 'You are talking weird.'

Valen clasped his hands together and continued murmuring the words. A moment later, he spread his fingers, opened his eyes, and spoke a single word.

Tip-tap, tip-tap.

'Get back, Gracie!' Chloe shouted, pulling her back to the couch.

'It's OK,' Valen said, raising a finger. 'It's just Little Henry coming alive. He is harmless, trust me.'

With wide eyes, Alexa spoke words native to her western land.

One by one, Henry's glass eyes lit up and shone a bright red. Each metal leg twitched, stretched out, then delicately touched the surface. Suddenly, the spider's body lifted off the table and Henry tip-tapped, dancing around in a circle.

'It's alive,' Gracie whispered. 'How is it alive?'

A sudden buzz of wings made Chloe and Gracie duck. Jay, the bumblebee, buzzed around the room. After two fast laps, he stopped in front of Gracie and buzzed angrily.

'Come here, Jay,' Valen said, holding out a finger.

Jay backed away from Gracie and landed on Valen's finger.

'Are you some kind of wizard?' Gracie said, her eyes as wide as saucers. 'How are you doing it? How are you making them live?'

'Just something I learnt from Dr Viktor,' Valen said with a wry smile. 'It's a gift I have.'

'But how?' Alexa said.

'That I cannot tell you,' Valen said. 'It is a secret of the old ways. I am bound by oath to never tell.'

'Are they safe?' Chloe said, peering closely at Jay.

'They are,' Valen said. 'Unless I don't want them to be.'

Gracie wrestled away from Chloe's grip and stood next to the desk. Little Henry turned and waved his blunt jaws at her.

'Go on,' Valen said. 'He won't hurt you.'

With a trembling finger, Gracie stretched out her hand. Little Henry waved a leg at her, then stood still. Gracie touched the top of Little Henry's body. The spider shuddered, tip-tapped his legs, then spun around in a neat circle.

'He is cute,' Gracie said with a smile.

Little Henry spun faster and faster until his legs couldn't keep up. With a clack-clack of his jaws, he lost his footing and spun in a blur of shiny metal.

Gracie lifted her hand to her mouth and giggled.

Chloe sat back on the couch and placed her leg over the armrest. The leather squeaked at the bouncing of her leg. She eyed Valen with suspicion.

'What?' Valen said, spreading his hands.

Chloe shook her head but said nothing.

'You are going to use the beasties to biff the guards?' Gracie said.

Valen chuckled. 'These little guys can create a distraction. They can't really biff them, Gracie.'

'How do you know the guards will follow them?' Alexa said.

'I don't,' Valen said. 'They may ignore them altogether.'

'What about Sia?' Gracie said. 'Can you do the same thing with the snake? Can you make her come to life?'

'Yes, I can,' Valen said, picking up the unfinished snake. 'Do you think she will be better at causing a distraction?'

'I think so,' Gracie said, clapping her hands. 'I think Henry and Sia will cause most of the problems for the guards.'

Jay buzzed his wings.

'Sorry, Jay,' Gracie said, touching the little bee. 'I don't think you will scare them that much.'

Valen grinned at Gracie. 'He may not scare them, but he sure can sting them.'

Gracie's eyes widened as she pulled her hand back.

'Only if I tell him too, remember?' Valen said.

Suddenly, the front door shuddered with a flurry of loud knocks.

CHAPTER 4
DONTE

'Get out of here,' Valen hissed at the girls.

'Open this door,' the Captain shouted. 'Or I will break it down.'

Chloe and Alexa disappeared through the office windows. Gracie ran upstairs to climb out of the bedroom window and onto the rooftop.

'Hold on,' Valen said, walking towards the front door. 'I am coming.'

The door rattled again with the hammering. Valen grabbed the handle and opened the door. The Captain placed a hand on Valen's chest and barged in.

After a few steps backwards, Valen dug his heels in and shoved the Captain. 'I am warning you, Captain. Touch me again and you won't leave this shop in one piece.'

'Where are they?' the Captain said, moving around Valen. 'We heard women's voices in here.'

'I don't know what you are talking about,' Valen said, placing a hand on the counter to block the Captain.

'Search the place,' the Captain said, waving his guards in.

'Where are you hiding your little friend, Valen?' Dec said as he walked in. 'You know we will find her.'

Valen kept his hand on the counter. 'None of you are going anywhere beyond this room.'

The Captain walked over to a shelf and tipped a box so its contents fell to the ground. 'We are here on Hargreaves's orders. You will let us look or we will take you to jail.'

With his eyes narrowing, Valen slowly removed his arm. 'I won't forget this, Captain. Break anything of value and I will make you all pay.'

Jon walked in behind Dec and snarled in Valen's face. 'You should not have come to Fairacre, outsider. And don't you threaten our captain.'

More guards poured into the shop. Valen backtracked up to his office and leant against the doorframe. He folded his arms and bared his teeth at anyone who came near him.

After the guards had completely gone through the shop, the Captain stood in front of Valen and waved a hand. 'Move aside.'

'These are my private quarters,' Valen said. 'You can search the shop, but not my home.'

The Captain reached for his rusting metal cuffs hanging from his belt. 'I am warning you, outsider. I will cuff you and take you to prison.'

Valen leant down and growled in the Captain's face. 'I don't care. You are not going into my private quarters. You can try to arrest me. And I will not hold myself responsible for the damage I do to your face.'

'As you wish,' the Captain said, taking a step backwards and waving his hand. 'Gentlemen, if you please.'

Guards with wooden batons rushed Valen. Valen reached down the side of his door and grabbed his club. A sickening crunch sounded through the shop as the club connected with the first guard's jaw. The guards paused for a second, then exploded in a roar of anger. Valen swung his club and caught a few more. In close quarters, though, there was only so much he could do before the guards piled on top of him. A minute later, he sat on the couch with his hands bound behind his back.

'Search everywhere,' the Captain said. 'You two, get upstairs.'

Two guards made their way upstairs. Valen lifted his chin in defiance as the guards ransacked his office.

'Where are they?' the Captain said, kicking Valen in the shins. 'Tell me or I will go to the jail, and I will hurt their leader.'

'You are an animal,' Valen said. 'I don't know where anyone is. Do you think they would be stupid enough to tell me anything?'

'They are women,' the Captain said. 'Yes, I believe they would tell you where they hide.'

'You underestimate them, Captain,' Valen said, the corners of his mouth turning up. 'One day, they will make you pay for your ignorance.'

The Captain burst out laughing, sending spittle in Valen's face. 'How? How are they going to make me pay? They can't even look after themselves. Why do you think we call them the sewer rats?'

'Thieves and murderers, they are,' Dec said.

'Diseased and filthy,' Jon said.

'Where are they, outsider?' the Captain said, kneeling. 'If they are not here, then they are in the sewers. We are very close to finding them. If you tell me how to get to them, I will make sure nobody gets hurt.'

'I don't know what you are talking about,' Valen said, shrugging. 'You have found nothing in my shop. It is time you left.'

The Captain stood up and shook his head at Valen. 'We had high hopes for you, outsider. We thought you would be a respected man in this town. Now look at you. A sewer-rat sympathiser.'

Valen looked up at the Captain. 'I do what is right.'

'You don't know what is right,' the Captain said. 'You are weak and you don't belong in this town.'

'There is nothing upstairs, Captain,' the guard said, entering the kitchen and looking into the office.

'Did the boy on the roof see or catch anything?' the Captain said.

'Don't know, sir,' the guard said. 'Will speak to him once we leave.'

The Captain took one last look at Valen then twirled his finger in the air. 'Let's get out of here, boys. It seems our big friend here has had a lucky escape.'

The guards walked out of the shop, leaving just the Captain, Dec and Jon.

'This is your last warning, outsider,' the Captain said. 'Mr Hargreaves and I will not tolerate any more of this. Step out of line and you will go to jail for a very long time.'

Valen stared unblinkingly at the Captain.

'Nothing to say?' the Captain said, tilting his head to one side.

Silence hung thick and threatening through the shop.

Dec raised an eyebrow at Jon, then snorted at Valen. 'Big man ain't that big now, is he?'

'OK, outsider,' the Captain said. 'We are leaving. I am sure you will get out of those bonds.'

'How?' Valen shouted after them. 'How am I going to get out of these bonds?'

Jon and Dec both chuckled.

The Captain looked over his shoulder and smiled. 'You will manage. Have a good day, sir.'

The shop door slammed shut. Valen struggled with his bonds, but they didn't budge.

Tip-tap, tip-tap.

On the floor in front of Valen, Little Henry danced around in small circles.

'Get him up here, Jay, you lazy bee,' Valen said. 'Go on, get him up here.'

Jay buzzed into life. He swooped down on Little Henry and lifted him into the air. With an angry buzz, Jay flew behind Valen and let Henry go. The small spider dropped in a heap. Click clack went his jaws. The bonds on Valen's wrists fell free.

'Thank you, Little Henry,' Valen said, looking over his shoulders. He stood and rubbed his wrists while shaking his head at the carnage in his office. Suddenly, the front door opened. Valen reached for his club.

'It is me, Valen,' Chloe said, walking through the shop. 'Are you OK?'

'Yes,' Valen said, dropping his club. 'Are all of you OK?'

'Have you seen Gracie?' Chloe said, her eyebrows raised in concern.

Valen frowned. 'Why would I have seen her? She went up through the bedroom window.'

'We cannot find her,' Chloe said. 'She didn't meet us at the meeting point.'

'You don't think—' Valen said, his voice wavering. 'You don't think they have her?'

Chloe shook her head. 'I don't think the Captain would have taken her. They would have made it very clear to Fairacre that they had caught her. She would have been paraded on the stairs of the town hall.'

Valen sank into the couch. 'Then where? Who else would take her? She wouldn't just disappear on her own, would she?'

Alexa walked up through the shop. 'I think we have found her, miss.'

'Where?' Chloe said, spinning around.

'It seems someone has taken her to Donte's,' Alexa said.

Chloe ran her hand through her locs. 'That is bad news. We cannot get her. Donte's is one of the most secured places in Fairacre.'

'How did she get caught?' Valen said, concern creasing his face.

'Donte has a group of men who capture these girls,' Chloe said. 'He has them prowling the streets constantly.'

'Or the guards caught her and handed her to Donte,' Alexa said. 'They do that sometimes to dodge any type of paperwork.'

Chloe bit her bottom lip. 'I doubt they would have handed over someone as important as Gracie. They would have definitely paraded her.'

'I don't understand why she won't escape,' Valen said. 'She isn't one to be afraid of being threatened.'

'When Donte has them, he makes it clear that if they try to escape, he will hurt the other girls,' Alexa said.

'So threatening the other girls to keep everyone in line?' Valen said. 'He is a sick man.'

Chloe nodded. 'Gracie won't do anything that may cause harm to the other girls.'

'We need to get those girls away from that man,' Valen said.

'We would, but we don't have space for all of them in the sewers,' Alexa said.

Valen suddenly stood and looked Chloe straight in the eye. 'I am going to get Gracie.'

'What do you mean?' Chloe said, raising both eyebrows. 'I don't think it's a good idea.'

Valen turned on his heel and made up the stairs to his bedroom. A few moments later, he came down wearing a set of leather armour. Over his armour, he wore a large cloak with a hood. He grabbed his club and signalled for Chloe to move out of the way.

'Valen, this isn't smart,' Chloe said. 'At least wait for nightfall.'

'I am not waiting for them to hurt Gracie,' Valen said. 'I have had enough of this, so please move out of my way.'

'You know we cannot wait for you,' Chloe said, spreading her hands. 'If they catch you, they will come here looking for us.'

'You won't need to be here,' Valen said. 'Just be near on the rooftops so you can take Gracie.'

Chloe stepped aside. 'We will be ready. But please be careful.'

Valen opened the door, took one last look at Chloe and Alexa, then stepped out into the setting afternoon sun.

The weaving-district streets were quiet. Shop owners had made themselves scarce after the Captain had made his presence in the weaving district known. Instead of turning right up the road, Valen turned left and walked towards Fairacre's southern wall. Once there, Valen followed the wall until he reached the south-west corner of Fairacre. He turned north and began the walk up the eastern wall. Up ahead, the eastern gate loomed. A few paces away, he crouched against the wall and counted four guards. He stayed crouched while he waited for an opening. After a few minutes, the guards left their posts and began inspecting a wagon full of orchard goods. Valen stood and strode across the east–west road and into the north-eastern district. He glanced over his shoulder to check if anyone was following. The wall brushed his right shoulder as he continued moving north. The sun set, leaving long shadows across the roads and walls of the north-eastern district. After walking halfway up the length of the eastern wall, Valen turned onto a dark cobblestone road. Halfway up the road, Donte's mansion sat with its doors firmly closed. On either side of the door were guards. One smoked. The other slept with his chin bouncing off his chest. Valen knelt and listened. From a window above the guards, the wail of a girl broke the silence.

Valen stood and walked up to the guards. He kicked the sleeping one. 'I am here to see Donte.'

The guard startled awake. 'Donte don't be taking visitors after dark. Go home.'

'I said I want to see Donte.' Valen leant in and jabbed the guard in the chest.

The guard drew his sword.

'I wouldn't do that, young man,' Valen said, lifting his cloak to show the guard his club.

'I said you need to leave,' the man said, pointing his sword at Valen.

Valen elbowed the guard in the nose, then spun and connected his fist against the head of the guard who smoked. Both men crumpled into a heap on the floor. Valen moved them aside, walked up the steps, and tried the door-handle. It sat firmly locked.

He ran a finger along the thick oak door frame. 'Let's try the old-fashioned way,' he said, banging his club against the door.

Footsteps echoed throughout the house.

A moment later, at eye height, a small thin panel on the door flew open. 'What do you want?' a woman said.

Valen gave the woman his best smile. 'I am here to see Donte. I am an old friend.'

'Donte not be telling me of any visitors coming here tonight,' the woman said.

'Does Donte ever remember when he is going to have visitors?' Valen said, widening his best smile.

The woman's eyes narrowed. She slammed back the viewing panel. Valen's shoulders slumped. Suddenly, the turning of locks echoed from the other side. The door cracked open. Valen slammed his full weight against it. With a bang, the door stopped. A thick chain held it partially closed.

'Donte!' the woman screamed.

Valen took a step back and again slammed his full weight into the door. The screw holding the chain to the wall popped out. The door hit the woman square in the face. With a thud, the woman landed on her backside and stared with a dazed look at Valen. From all corners of the house, Valen heard footsteps charging towards him.

A man appeared at the end of the long passageway. 'What do you want?' he said, wielding a knife at Valen. 'How dare you break into Donte's home!'

Valen strode up the passage. 'Where is she?' he thundered.

The man, seeing the club, took a step back. 'Where is who?'

'The girl they just brought in this afternoon,' Valen said. 'Where is she?'

Footsteps from around the house grew louder.

The man waved his knife at Valen's face.

Valen flicked his club and caught the man's nose. Blood splattered onto the man's shirt. His eyes rolled back into his head as he slumped to the floor.

'Intruder!' the woman shouted.

Valen reached into his pocket and pulled out a little round ball. 'Find her,' Valen said, throwing Jay up into the air.

Jay buzzed back down the passageway. At the first door, he flew to the ground and crawled under.

A score of men appeared from corridors branching off the main passageway. Valen sneered at the men as he bounced his club in his hand. With a shout to battle, the men charged. One by one, the guards crumpled to the ground as the club crunched into their heads. The house fell into silence. The sobbing of young girls sounded from all the doors along the corridor. Valen closed his eyes and brought his rage under control. Jay appeared in front of him.

'You have found her?' he said.

Jay buzzed in a circle, then disappeared down an adjacent corridor. Valen followed until Jay stopped at the second-to-last door.

'This one?'

Jay buzzed in another circle.

With one swift kick, Valen broke the door off its hinges.

'Well, it's about time,' Gracie said, standing with her arms folded. 'And you could have warned me. What if I was listening with my head against the door?'

Valen walked over to Gracie. 'Are you OK?'

'Oh, I am just fine,' Gracie said, a small stab of pain creasing over her face. 'You should see what the others look like.'

A smile appeared on Valen's face. 'I should have known you were going to give them a hard time.'

'Didn't stand a chance,' Gracie said, while gingerly taking a step forward.

Valen turned to walk out of the door. 'Come on, let's get going.'

'I can't leave,' Gracie said.

Valen spun around. 'What do you mean?'

'They will hurt the other girls if I disappear,' Gracie said. 'There are so many girls, Valen.'

'You can't stay here,' Valen said.

An eyebrow shot up into Gracie's fringe. 'Oh, can't I?'

Valen walked back to Gracie and knelt on one knee. 'I know this is hard, but you can do more good out there than you can in here.'

Gracie lifted a defiant chin.

'I promise I will help you get these girls out of here one day,' Valen said. 'We just cannot do it now.'

'You swear?' Gracie said. 'You promise, swear on your beasties' lives?'

'I do,' Valen said. 'But you need to come with me before more guards get here.'

A grimace of pain spread across Gracie's face. She felt her side.

'What is wrong?' Valen said.

'It is nothing,' Gracie said. 'They just beat me, that's all. They never go for the face, otherwise people in the town would see and they would get annoyed.'

A long growl came out of Valen's mouth. 'I am going to kill this man.'

'Who, Donte?' Gracie said. 'Take a ticket and wait in line, big man. There is a long list of us who want to get rid of him.'

Footsteps sounded in the rooms above them.

'Come on,' Valen said, grabbing Gracie's hand. 'Time to move.'

Gracie sucked in a mouthful of air.

'Sorry, Gracie,' Valen said. 'But we really need to move.'

They followed Jay down the corridor. At the end, Valen turned right and made for the front door.

'Hey, you!' a man shouted. 'I am going to tell Mr Hargreaves that it was you who broke into my house.'

Valen spun around and stared at the thickset man with jewels on his fingers. 'Are you Donte?' he said.

'Yes, I am Donte. What are you doing with that girl?'

'I am going to put you deep in the ground,' Valen said, taking a step forward. 'So deep, nobody will ever find you.'

A look of alarm spread across Donte's face. He took a step backwards, then disappeared down a corridor.

'Come on,' Gracie said, grabbing Valen's hand and pulling him towards the door. 'You won't find him in this maze of a house.'

Valen followed Gracie out into the night. 'Go left towards the eastern wall. We need to get to the southern district.'

As Gracie turned left, a soft whistle from the rooftops broke the quiet night.

Valen looked up. Chloe stood on the rooftop, looking down at them. Valen smiled and gave her a thumbs-up. With a roll of her eyes, Chloe pointed towards the east wall. Valen nodded, then hurried along the street. Gracie took in sharp breaths as she skipped along.

Just before they reached the eastern wall, Chloe stepped out from an alley. 'You crazy man,' she said, eyeballing Valen. 'You could have got yourself and Gracie killed.'

'But he didn't,' Gracie said, holding onto her side. 'I am not dead. I am fine, see?'

Chloe knelt and pulled Gracie's top up so she could see her ribs. 'They have broken your ribs. You are definitely not fine.'

'I am going to kill him,' Valen said, his snarl sounding feral. 'My club will take his head from his shoulders.'

Chloe smirked. 'I have no doubt one day you will. But not today.'

'Can you get home from here?' Valen said, squinting down the dark alley.

'We can go through the sewers,' Chloe said. 'What are you going to do?'

'I will be fine,' Valen said. 'Make sure you get to safety and get Gracie's ribs looked at. If you need a person to help with that injury, I can find someone.'

Chloe took a step forward and placed a hand on Valen's chest. 'Thank you for getting her back.'

Valen turned a light pink. 'Best you get going. Everyone will be searching for me soon.'

'Be safe,' Chloe said, turning into the alley. Valen smiled as the girls disappeared into the darkness.

With Fairacre's eastern wall to his left, Valen retraced his steps until he reached the eastern gate. The guards sat around a small fire playing dice. Valen pulled his cloak over his head and crossed the road. He continued to follow the southern wall until he reached the street leading to his shop. He walked up to the door and swung it open. Valen shivered at the lack of a doorbell sound. Without turning lights on, he made his way down to his office. He bent over and picked up his office chair. Next, he picked up and righted his desk.

'You best not have damaged my tools, Captain,' Valen said under his breath. He opened the desk drawer and reached deep inside until he felt the familiar cloth that surrounded his tools. He pulled the small bag free, then sank into his groaning office chair.

'Time to get you finished,' Valen said, reaching up to the shelf and picking up the half-done snake. Little Henry, with his red eyes, appeared and danced on the tabletop. Jay remained quiet in Valen's pocket.

'What do you want?' Valen said, looking at Little Henry.

Little Henry tip-tapped on the desk then spun around in a circle. Valen picked up a bent tube from the floor. He removed his tools from their bag and lay them in a row on the table. The chair creaked as he spun around, looking for his eyeglass. On the floor, near the couch, lay the unbroken magnifying glass. He stretched over, picked up the eyeglass, and placed it next to his tools.

'Now keep quiet, you hear,' Valen said, waving a finger at Little Henry. 'I need to concentrate.'

Little Henry spread his eight legs, so his body dropped onto the table.

Valen closed his eyes and began the chant Dr Viktor had taught him. A few moments later, a glimmer of blue light surrounded his hands. Continuing the chant, Valen picked up his tools and started working on the snake. His hands took on a life of their own as he deftly cut, moulded and attached the fine slivers of tubing to the snake. An hour later, Valen placed a small crystal into the second eye socket. He stopped the chant and laid down his tools. The dim blue light faded. 'Now for the transference of my essence,' he said.

Little Henry lifted his body off the table and looked at Valen expectantly.

Valen closed his eyes and began another chant. A few moments later, he released a small ball of his own internal essence, which travelled into the snake. Valen shivered. He would never get used to the way he felt during and after releasing a small piece of his soul into his little beasts.

The eyes on the snake flashed alive. With a hiss, Sia propped herself up to her full height and showed Valen her long, thin fangs.

'Hello, little one,' Valen said, holding out his hand.

Sia slithered up his arm and around his thick neck.

'I think it is time we go and save a dear friend,' Valen said. 'What do you think, Sia?'

Sia's eyes gleamed as she swayed her head at Valen.

CHAPTER 5

THE BIG RED BARN

Valen looked up into the clear night sky and took a deep breath. He pulled the hood of his cloak over his head and tied the fasteners together. The one light on his cobblestone street flickered on and off, on and off. With his trusty club hanging from his belt, he marched up the winding street. Sia slithered around his neck and kept her head resting on his shoulder. Little Henry poked his head out of his breast pocket and Jay buzzed about angrily, darting here and there.

Valen made his way north, towards the east–west road. As he got closer, he increased his stride, making it harder for people to speak to him. He entered the east–west road and turned towards the town square. With his head held high, he stayed in the middle of the road so nobody could mistake him for someone else.

'Where are you going, outsider?' a man said from his shop door.

Valen passed him before the question ended. He continued striding towards the town square. Halfway up the road, two guards walking in the opposite direction stopped and glared at him. Sia raised her head off Valen's shoulder and hissed. With wide eyes, the guards pulled their swords. Valen raised a surprised eyebrow at the guards' bravery. With a roar, he ran at them, sending his cloak flapping in the wind. Jay darted ahead of Valen and buzzed angrily around the guards' heads.

'Stop,' a guard said, holding out his hand.

Before the second guard could say anything, Valen ploughed into both of them, sending them flying across the street. One guard lay still, with a trickle of blood dripping from his head. The other raised his hand to his mouth and whistled.

'That's going to waken everyone, Jay,' Valen said, as he jogged towards the square. 'Are you three ready for some fun?'

Jay buzzed, Henry clacked and Sia hissed.

Two more guards jumped out of the alleys. Valen pounded one to the ground while Jay stung the other.

He walked across the square and made for the back of the town hall, where a wide stone staircase led down into the ground. Double-stepping down the steps, Valen stopped just short of the massive wrought-iron gate. Two guards sat on either side. Without waiting for the guards to say something, Valen swung his club and knocked one of them unconscious. He picked up the second guard and slammed him against the gate.

'Open this gate or I will make sure the same thing happens to the two of you,' he said, eyeing the two guards on the inside.

One guard shied away, but the second guard stood firm. 'Pray tell, how are you going to open the gate?' the guard said. 'I am the only one with the keys.'

A smile stretched across Valen's face. 'Thank you kindly for the information, sir.'

The guard gave Valen a confused look.

'Off you go, you three,' Valen said.

Jay flew at the guard and stung him on the cheek. Sia wrapped around the guard's feet. He let out a scream as he collapsed to the ground. Little Henry jumped onto the guard and waved his front legs at him. The guard let out another scream of terror.

'Stop playing with him, you lot,' Valen said. 'Bring me the keys.'

Little Henry scuttled all over the guard until he found his keys. He dislodged them, then moved aside as Sia slithered over and grabbed them in her jaws. With a hiss, she slithered over to Valen and dropped the keys.

Valen threw the guard to one side. He picked up the keys and unlocked the gate. The last guard, with wide eyes, sat cowering against the wall.

'Get out of here,' Valen said, holding the gate open. 'If you tell anyone I am here, I will find you.'

The guard slunk out of the gate and ran up the stairs.

Valen closed the gate behind him and double-stepped his way down the stairs into the jail. At the bottom, another set of iron gates waited for him. He tried the other keys until one worked. He swung the gate open and walked into the quiet jail. Every cell was empty.

'What is going on?'

Quiet chattering at the far end of the jail broke the silence. Valen walked down the passage until he reached a metal gate that spanned the wall. He grabbed the handle and pulled. The gate stood firm. Valen tried the other keys until the lock clicked. He slid open the big gate and ducked just as an arrow whistled over his head.

'Do not come in here!' a guard shouted. 'There are eight of us and we will not hesitate to kill you.'

'Time to go to work,' Valen said. 'Off you go.'

Sia hissed and slithered off to where the voices had come from. Little Henry jumped from his pocket and landed in a heap. He pushed himself up and scampered off into the jails. Jay darted off with an angry buzz. Valen leant against the metal gate's frame and waited patiently. Suddenly, a blood-curdling scream sounded through the jail. Shortly after, another scream echoed. Valen waited a few more seconds, then charged in with his club held high. Another arrow shot past his face. Valen dropped and quickly surveyed the room. Jay buzzed over two men who lay on the ground writhing in pain. Two men were swinging their swords at a dancing Henry. A further guard gripped a hissing Sia as she squeezed his neck.

'One more left,' Valen said, just as an arrow pierced his leather armour. Hissing through his teeth, Valen grabbed the arrow and pulled it out of his shoulder. He scanned the jail, looking for the hidden guard. Down at the end of the corridor sat a couple of wooden barrels. The top of a guard's head was just visible.

'Jay, he is at the end of the jail. Get him,' Valen shouted.

Jay buzzed down the corridor towards the guard.

A scream sounded from behind the barrels. The guard came running out, swatting his hands at the buzzing bee. Jay dive-bombed the guard and stung him horribly around the face. Red welts sprang up over the guard's face and neck. Valen walked forward and struck him on the nose. The guard crumpled to the ground.

Valen counted six guards, which meant two were missing. He walked down another passage until he reached a big metal door.

Jay hovered in front of Valen.

'Yes, you can go in there,' Valen said.

Jay buzzed happily, then flew down to the bottom of the door, where he walked through the small gap.

'Anytime now,' Valen said, waiting patiently.

A scream sounded from inside the cell. The locks on the door slid back. A wild-eyed guard tried to barge through the door. Valen grabbed him by the collar and threw him back in. Little Henry scuttled past Valen and onto the guard's chest, where he danced in circles. The guard covered his eyes and started mumbling something Valen couldn't understand.

'Who is there?' Naomi said.

Valen walked past the metal door. 'Where are you, Naomi?'

'Down here,' Naomi said. 'The last cell.'

Valen walked down the row and saw a figure sitting with her back against the wall. His massive hands grabbed the cell door and rattled it.

'One of the guards has the key,' Naomi said as she pushed herself to a standing position.

Valen stopped rattling the door and stared at Naomi.

'It is nothing,' Naomi said. 'Just bruises and cuts. They will heal in time.'

'I will destroy them all,' Valen thundered, rattling the door. 'One by one, I will make them pay.'

'Over there, Valen,' Naomi said, pointing to the guard Jay had half-stung to death. 'The keys are on his belt.'

Valen stopped rattling the cell door and walked over to the guard. He felt inside the guard's pocket until he found the key. Shouts and footsteps echoed from the entrance of the jail.

'Hurry,' Naomi said. 'We can get out of here through the sewers.'

The door swung open. Naomi limped out of the cell and up to the big metal door, which she closed quietly. 'We can go through there,' she said, pointing to a grate in the wall.

Valen smirked. 'There is no way I am getting through there.'

'You are going to try,' Naomi said, matter-of-factly.

'I am too big, Naomi. Plus, I need to keep these guys busy,' Valen said, pointing at the closed door.

'I am not leaving you here,' Naomi said. 'We can get you through the grate. It will just take some time.'

'I will be fine,' Valen said. 'I will need to keep them busy to give you a head start.'

Naomi limped over to Valen and kissed him gently on the cheek. 'Thank you. I will come and get you. Be ready.'

Valen walked up to the grate and ripped it off the wall. 'Go.'

'Be ready,' Naomi said, as her head disappeared into the sewers. 'Do you hear me, Valen? Be ready.'

Valen placed the grate back into the hole. Fists pounded on the big metal door.

'Open up!' a man shouted.

'Nobody is home,' Valen replied.

'Who is that?' the guard shouted.

Valen walked back to the cell Naomi had been in. He swung the door closed. With a flick of his wrist, he threw the key at the guard lying motionless on the ground. He moved into the shadows and sat with his back to the wall.

After a few moments, the cell door slammed open and in poured a stream of guards.

'Where is he?' a guard shouted.

'Time to hide, you three,' Valen said, waving his hand at his beasts.

Sia, Jay and Little Henry slunk off into the darkness. Valen watched the guards scramble around the jail as they searched for him.

One stopped at his cell and peered in. 'She is still here.'

The Captain entered the jail. 'What is going on?'

'He isn't here, Captain,' a guard said.

'What are you on about?' the Captain said. 'Who did this damage to your pathetic brothers, then? Of course he is in here.'

The guards looked at each other in confusion.

The Captain walked up to Valen's cell. He looked in and chuckled. 'Very clever, outsider.'

'Do you think?' Valen said. 'It seems your guards need to go back to school.'

'You don't have to tell me that,' the Captain said. 'Not much between the ears.'

Valen steeled himself with some deep breaths.

'You,' the Captain said. 'Get me that key that is next to that guard.'

The guard retrieved the key and handed it to the Captain.

'That's the only smart thing you have done all day,' the Captain muttered. He turned the lock and swung open the gate.

'Gentlemen, if you please,' the Captain said, looking at his guards.

A stream of guards piled into the cell. Valen curled into a ball as a stream of fists and punches rained down on him.

'Why are you not fighting back?' one guard said.

'He is keeping us distracted,' the Captain said. 'No sign of the sewer-rat leader, is there? Very smart, isn't he?'

The guards stopped hitting Valen and again looked around in confusion.

'You have got to be kidding me,' the Captain said, raising his eyes to the ceiling. 'The girls belong to a group, gentlemen. What is that group called?'

'Sewer rats, sir,' one guard said, after thinking for a second.

'Yes,' the Captain said, jabbing his finger against the guard's head. 'Because they live in the sewers, right?'

After another few seconds, the guard's eyes widened as he realised. 'Check the place for access to the sewers.'

'Finally,' the Captain said, throwing his hands up in the air.

'Must be hard being you,' Valen said, as he spat blood against the wall.

'Oh, you have no idea,' the Captain said, shaking his head. 'I have seen children with bigger brains.'

'Found it!' a guard shouted.

'Well?' the Captain said, raising an eyebrow at the guard.

'We go down there?' the guard said, peering through the grate.

'For the love of all things sacred,' the Captain said. 'Yes, you go down there, you imbecile.'

Valen smiled as the guards removed the grate and struggled to get down through the hole.

'I miss the City of Lynn,' the Captain said.

'So what's next?' Valen said.

The Captain swung the grate closed. 'Looks like you have found a new home, outsider. See you around.'

Valen stood and walked to the bars. 'Aren't you going to take me to Mr Hargreaves?'

The Captain ignored him and walked out of the jail.

As day four dawned, a red glow played through the window into Valen's cell. Two days ago, Little Henry had tried to break through the lock, but his jaws couldn't get through the steel. The Captain had placed a guard in the room and now didn't bother closing the main jail door. Valen moved himself to the small straw bed in the corner. His wounds were healing and the aches and pains subsiding.

'What do you think they are going to do with you?' the guard said, throwing a die against the wall.

Valen ignored the guard.

'It's been four days and you haven't said anything,' the guard said. 'If you don't talk soon, they will just lose patience and hang you.'

'I will talk when I need to,' Valen said.

'Ahh, day four and he talks,' the guard said, throwing another set of dice.

'You must have done something terrible for the Captain to give you this job,' Valen said.

The guard chuckled. 'Was late for duty. There is this girl in the weaving district. I am saving up to buy her, but we couldn't wait any longer to see each other.'

Valen placed his head back on the wall and let out a long sigh.

'None of this would have happened if you had just chosen someone to be your wife,' the guard said. 'What is wrong with you? Couldn't find someone you liked?'

'There is a difference between choosing and buying,' Valen muttered.

'Same difference if you ask me,' the guard said.

'And how are we today?' the Captain said, walking into the jail.

The guard scrambled to his feet. 'He has been behaving, sir. He actually talked.'

'Did he now?' the Captain said, placing his hands on his hips. 'He usually likes to talk with that big club of his, don't you, outsider? Put a lot of my men in the hospital, didn't you?'

The guard sniggered. 'Can't be doing much clubbing when stuck behind these bars, can he, sir?'

'No, he cannot,' the Captain said.

Valen kept his mouth shut.

'We are going for a walk, outsider,' the Captain said, signalling to the guard to open the gate. 'It seems Hargreaves has decided what he wants to do with you.'

'It's a hanging, isn't it, sir?' the guard said, as he rattled the key in the lock. 'We all love a bit of a hanging, don't we, sir?'

'I have asked for a hanging,' the Captain said. 'But Hargreaves has got soft after he met that Petra woman. So I am not so sure anymore.'

'He will lose the next mayor elections if he stays soft, won't he, sir?' the guard said, swinging open the jail gate.

'Not if the rich northern district has anything to say about it,' the Captain said, stepping aside. 'Come on, let's get this outsider into handcuffs then get him topside.'

'Turn around if you will, outsider,' the guard said.

Valen glared at the guard.

'Come on now, Valen,' the Captain said. 'It's no use prolonging the inevitable.'

'Boo,' Valen shouted at the guard.

The guard jumped two feet into the air.

'For the love of—' the Captain said, shaking his head. 'Can you stop toying with my boys? Look how scared they are.'

Valen smirked, turned around, and placed his hands behind his back. The cold steel bit into his wrists, then locked with a click. The guard spun Valen around and presented him to the Captain.

'Let's go,' the Captain said with a nod.

The guard led Valen through the jail towards the exit.

'I would close your eyes when we get to the surface,' the Captain said. 'You haven't seen the sun for four days and it will burn them.'

Valen closed his eyes as they exited the jail. After a few moments, he opened them slowly and grimaced as the painful sun still burnt through his retinas.

'Lead him,' the Captain said. 'He can't see anything.'

The guard walked them around the town hall and into the square. 'Doesn't look like a hanging to me,' he said.

'I told you,' the Captain said. 'Hargreaves has turned soft in his old age. Remember to tell all your friends.'

Valen stumbled up the stairs and into the town hall. The guard led him into the middle of the hall and sat him on a lone chair.

'Sit and make yourself comfortable,' the Captain said.

Valen sat and blinked to get his eyesight back.

About fifteen minutes later, Mr Hargreaves appeared out of the offices and walked over to where Valen sat. 'Get me a chair, won't you please?' he said, nodding to the guard.

'Yes, Mr Mayor,' the guard said, jogging off to the offices.

'I trust the Captain has been treating you well?' Mr Hargreaves said.

Valen stared at Mr Hargreaves.

'Hasn't been the talking type of late,' the Captain said.

The guard jogged back to the centre of the town hall and placed a chair opposite Valen.

'These guards have all asked for you to be hanged by the neck,' Mr Hargreaves said as he sat.

'Hanged till he can breathe no more,' the guard said. 'He deserves it for freeing the sewer-rat leader.'

'But there won't be a hanging,' Mr Hargreaves said, ignoring the guard.

Valen sat motionless, his stare piercing into Mr Hargreaves.

'What we are going to do,' Mr Hargreaves said, 'is banish you from Fairacre.'

'What do you mean, banish me from Fairacre?' Valen said. 'This is my home.'

'The Captain will escort you out of Fairacre immediately,' Mr Hargreaves said, lifting his chin. 'He will escort you to a gate of your choice. Once you step through the gate, you can consider yourself banned from Fairacre forever.'

Valen's eyes narrowed. A muscle in his jaw twitched. He snarled at Mr Hargreaves.

'And you will not have the luxury of going to your shop before you go,' Mr Hargreaves said. 'What you have on your back is what you will leave with.'

'That is theft,' Valen said. 'I have worked hard to create that shop, and its contents are mine.'

'Should have thought about that when you were playing with the sewer rats now, shouldn't you?' the guard chuckled.

'Keep your mouth shut,' the Captain said, slapping the back of the guard's head.

'Captain,' Mr Hargreaves said. 'Please escort Valen out of Fairacre.'

Valen struggled against the metal cuffs. 'You will pay for this, Hargreaves. You spineless fool. This is criminal.'

The Captain grabbed Valen and pulled him to his feet. 'Come on, sunshine. Time for you to go for a very long walk to somewhere nobody cares about.'

'I will not go without getting my things out of the shop,' Valen said.

'Yes, you will,' Mr Hargreaves said, rising from his chair. 'Or I will make sure we hang every sewer rat we catch. Get out of my city, Valen.'

'You coward,' Valen said. 'All those women ever wanted is a fair chance at life.'

'That is not for you to determine,' Mr Hargreaves said, turning and walking back to his office. 'Captain, if you will.'

The Captain shoved Valen towards the town hall doors. 'Come on, time to move.'

Valen stumbled forward as he struggled with his bonds.

'Which gate?' the Captain said.

Valen remained quiet.

'I said, which gate? Choose or I will choose for you.'

'Southern gate,' Valen said.

They left the town hall and entered the southern street. The Captain marched Valen down the cobbled road. At the market stalls, Greta stopped sweeping and spat on the ground in front of the Captain.

A guard lifted a hand to strike her, but Greta slunk away into an alley.

Valen scanned the rooftops. No sewer rats looked back.

'Look here, Jon,' Dec said. 'It's the outsider. Why is he here?'

'Banished,' the guard said. 'He isn't being hanged.'

'Lucky,' Dec said. 'Hargreaves is getting soft.'

'I can smell him from here,' Jon said, waving a hand in front of his face.

'Even Greta smells better than this sewer-rat-loving scum,' Dec said. 'We should hang you, but good riddance, I say.'

The Captain marched Valen through the southern gate and brought them to a halt on the other side of the drawbridge. He pulled out a metal key and undid the cuffs. Valen rubbed his wrists to get the blood flowing.

'It is a sad day for me,' the Captain said, as he placed his cuffs on his belt. 'On the one hand, I think you would have been a great ally and defender of Fairacre. And, on the other hand, I don't get to hang you for being a traitor.'

'Sometimes you cannot have everything you want,' Valen said, as he cast his eyes south.

'Where will you go?' the Captain said.

'I don't know,' Valen said.

The Captain took a step back, turned, and walked back over the drawbridge.

Valen didn't look back. He set off left and followed the dirt road running alongside the moat. To his right lay fields of wheat. In the distance sat a big red barn.

Valen stopped at a road leading south. He stared at the big red barn. 'Our first stop, little ones,' he said.

Little Henry clacked his jaws. Jay buzzed out of his pocket and darted towards the barn. Sia hissed and snapped her jaws.

CHAPTER 6
INTO THE DEPTHS

The barn door rumbled open. 'Where are you?' the farmer said.

'I am here,' Valen said, walking around the hay bales. 'What do you need?'

'Get this hay onto that wagon over there if you can,' the farmer said. 'I need to get this shipped to the City of Lynn tomorrow morning.'

'Yes, sir,' Valen said, picking up the pitchfork. 'I will finish it before nightfall.'

'I have brought dried meats and bread for you,' the farmer said, pointing to the bag on the wagon seat.

'Thank you, sir,' Valen said.

'I will be back just before nightfall to pick up the trailer,' the farmer said. 'Any trouble, I will be across the way.'

Valen watched the man walk into the fields. He picked up the pitchfork and began loading the hay onto the wagon. Jay buzzed around his head as he worked. At midday, Valen stopped loading the hay and sat on the seat of the wagon. He opened up the bag and pulled out the bread and meats. Little Henry poked out of his breast pocket and waved a few legs.

'You don't need any of this,' Valen said, tapping Little Henry on the head.

Little Henry shuffled back into Valen's pocket.

Valen put a piece of bread in his mouth, then froze. He turned and watched a group of girls walk up the southern path. They stopped at the barn to gather water out of the rain catcher.

'Who do you think is going to choose me?' a tall girl said as she dunked a bottle into the barrel.

'You are an expert fruit picker,' another girl said. 'Maybe a man who owns orchards?'

'I really hope so,' the tall girl said with a smile. 'It is so nice to be out of that school, isn't it?'

'I will miss Miss Petra though.'

'So will I,' the tall girl said.

'You were always her favourite.'

'No, I wasn't,' the tall girl said. 'That young girl, Juno, who I taught to pick fruit, is definitely her favourite.'

'Do you think she will do a good job at running the orchard?' the girl said.

'She will, I am sure. This last year she even made her own fruit-picking basket.'

'Dedicated.'

'What about you?' the tall girl said. 'Do you think someone will pick you?'

'Someone has already picked me. My father picked him for me. I haven't met him yet.'

'So exciting. Look, there is the gate. Let's get our water and hurry into town.'

Valen watched the girls walk up the southern road. He brought a piece of meat up to his mouth then thought better of it. His appetite gone, he threw the meat back into the bag. In the distance, cheers sounded from the southern gate. Valen watched the girls walk over the drawbridge.

Clack-clack went Little Henry's jaws.

'What?' Valen said, angrily.

Little Henry jumped out of Valen's pocket and scuttled off into the barn.

Valen swung his legs off the wagon and dropped to the ground. He walked back to the barn, opened the door, and picked up his pitchfork. With seething anger pumping through his veins, he stabbed the fork as hard as he could into the hay. The hay flew into the back of the wagon. Valen worked until his muscles burnt like lava.

'Thanks, Valen,' the farmer said.

Valen waved goodbye, then turned and splashed the water from the rain catcher over his face. The moon cast a bright light across the wheat field. Valen checked to see he was alone, then stripped down to his underwear. He picked up a bucket, filled it with water, then dumped his dirty clothes into it. Once the clothes were clean, Valen hung each item along the fence.

Jay buzzed around his head.

'Yes, Jay, it is very undignified standing here in nothing but my underwear,' Valen said as the bumblebee hovered in front of him. 'But I refuse to live in dirty clothes.'

Sia slunk out of the grass, raised her head, and used her tongue to taste the air.

Valen walked over to the trough next to the rain catcher. 'Guard my clothes, Sia.'

The snake lowered her head and disappeared into the barn.

Valen shook his head at the retreating snake. He stepped into the trough and lowered his body into the cold water. His teeth chattered as he washed off the filth that caked his body. The water splashed out of the trough as he slipped underneath the surface to clean his hair.

'Enjoying yourself?' Chloe said, as Valen surfaced.

Valen burst into a coughing fit as he accidentally sucked in some water.

'Are you OK?' Chloe said, with a look of concern.

'Can you turn around, please?' Valen said, his voice hoarse.

Chloe smirked. 'Sure.'

He climbed out of the trough, grabbed his clothes, and dressed. 'You can turn around now,' he said, his teeth chattering.

'You look cold,' Chloe said, tilting her head to one side.

'I am cold,' Valen said, as he turned and walked into the barn. 'Coming?'

Chloe followed him into the barn and closed the door.

Valen walked to the back of the barn where he grabbed some dry straw and rubbed his clothes dry. 'What are you doing here?' he said, looking at Chloe.

'Do you think Naomi, Gracie and I were going to just let you disappear?'

'I was sort of hoping you would,' Valen said with a tinge of sadness. 'I am not the person to be seen with right now.'

'What, and lose our only male ally in Fairacre?' Chloe said, folding her arms. 'We need you.'

Valen sat on a hay bale. 'I am no longer a Fairacre resident, and I have lost everything.'

Chloe unfolded her arms and sat on the bale next to him. 'So fight to get it back.'

Valen snorted. 'That would mean a complete overthrow of all the rules in Fairacre.'

'Not exactly,' Chloe said. 'You just have to play them at their rules.'

'What do you mean?' Valen said.

'There is a way to play by their rules and not play by their rules,' Chloe said.

Valen went cross-eyed. 'Say that again?'

Chloe chuckled. 'You go back into town and tell them you have seen the error of your ways. You tell them you are going to buy a wife. And you are also going to buy a house in the northern district.'

Valen stared at Chloe with his mouth open.

'You don't actually have to buy a wife,' Chloe said, shaking her head. 'Just pretend you are looking for the right one.'

Valen closed his mouth. 'I don't know if I can do that.'

'It's just pretend,' Chloe said. 'Think of the bigger picture.'

'This doesn't feel right,' Valen said.

Chloe stood and faced him. She grabbed both his hands and pulled him to his feet. With one hand wrapped around his neck, she drew him into a long kiss. Chloe took a step back. Valen blinked with shock.

'Hello, Valen,' Chloe said, tilting her head to one side.

Valen shook his head.

'Are you OK?' Chloe said.

He took a step forward and kissed her again.

'OK there,' Chloe said, pulling away. 'Let's take this slow, shall we?'

Valen dropped onto a bale of hay and stared into the night sky.

Chloe sat next to him and wrapped her arm around his waist.

'I liked that a lot,' Valen said.

'So did I,' Chloe said, smiling up at him.

'I still don't know if I can do this, Chloe,' Valen said. 'I am not sure I won't give myself away if I have to lie.'

Chloe stood up. 'I think I need to show you how important this is.'

Valen frowned. 'What do you mean?'

'I mean, for me to show you how important this is, I am going to break the rules and Naomi is going to be furious with me.'

'What do you mean?' Valen said.

'You seem to say that a lot, Valen,' Chloe said, grinning down at him. 'What I mean is, you are coming with me.'

A smirk played across Valen's face as he spread his hands and said, 'What do you mean?'

Her eyes rolling, Chloe grabbed Valen by the hand. 'We are going to visit the sewer rats.'

'You are going to take me to the sewers?' Valen said, stumbling after Chloe.

'Yes. There is an entrance near the southern gate,' Chloe said. 'It's a bit of a tight squeeze, but we should get you through.'

Valen opened his mouth to ask a question, then thought better of it.

'What?' Chloe said, blowing air out of her cheeks.

'Can I have another kiss before we go?' Valen said, his face turning pink.

Chloe stood on her toes and kissed him on the cheek. 'There,' she said. 'Now let's go. And please do everything I tell you to do from here on. It's really important.'

'OK,' Valen said, with a silly grin.

They walked to the barn door and peered out. The moon, still high in the sky, made it a little too bright for them to walk along the dirt roads.

'We cross the road and enter the wheat fields,' Chloe said. 'When in the fields, we need to keep our heads lower than the wheat.'

'I will try my best,' Valen said.

Chloe darted out of the barn and across the road. Valen followed close behind. The wheat swished as they both entered it.

'How far is it?' Valen whispered.

'It is to the left of the southern gate, so not too far,' Chloe said.

Valen kept close to Chloe as she wove through the wheat. About five minutes later, she stopped and sank to her belly. Valen crawled up next to her. The road ran east to west in front of them.

'You see that hole over there?' Chloe whispered, pointing to some bushes over the road.

'No,' Valen said, squinting.

'Well, it's there,' Chloe said. 'We need to get over this road without being seen.'

'We could just dash over?' Valen said.

'Too dangerous,' Chloe said. 'That entrance to the sewers is our escape route if the guards ever find us in the sewers. Showing them where it is now could mean the end of the sewer rats.'

'So how do we do this?' Valen said.

'We wait. When a cart comes past, we run over behind it.'

Valen placed his chin on his hands. The hypnotic swishing of the wheat made his eyes droop. He closed them and thought about Chloe. A small smile played across his face. Sleep took hold.

'Come on,' Chloe said, nudging him in the ribs.

Valen blinked awake. He jumped to his feet and followed Chloe behind the passing wagon. They darted to the other side of the road and jumped into the bushes.

'Did I fall asleep?' Valen said.

Chloe grinned. 'It is OK. I would have too if I was stuck living in that barn. Come on, we need to get you through this gate.'

Valen placed his hand on Chloe's shoulder and followed her into the darkness.

'Wait one minute while your eyes adjust,' Chloe said, stopping just before a rusted gate.

A few moments later, Valen made out the gate that lay over the entrance to the sewers. He crinkled his nose at the smell. 'It's disgusting.'

'You get used to it,' Chloe said as she grabbed the gate and pulled it open.

Valen's teeth ground together at the squealing noise it made. 'Aren't they going to hear it?'

Chloe shook her head. 'Sound travels out into the fields and not back into Fairacre. Can you squeeze through?'

Valen turned sideways and blew out all of his breath to make himself thinner. He cursed as every conceivable item of clothing caught on the sharp bits of the gate. Once inside, he gagged at the horrid smell.

'Do you need a moment?' Chloe said.

'I don't understand how you can live down here,' Valen said, his face turning green. 'It is truly disgusting.'

'The places we hide don't smell that bad,' Chloe said. 'It smells bad here because this is where all the sewage runs out.'

'I am getting used to it,' Valen said, breathing through his mouth.

'By the way, your beasties' eyes look dangerous in this light,' Chloe said, pointing to Sia's red eyes. 'Make sure they don't scare the children.'

'Come on, you lot,' Valen said, holding open his pockets. Jay and Henry disappeared inside them. Sia curled around Valen's neck and closed her eyes.

Chloe shook her head. 'I still cannot believe you bring life to metal objects. How do you do it?'

'A story for another time, perhaps,' Valen said. 'Lead the way.'

'Keep your hand against the wall,' Chloe said. 'In the middle of the tunnel, the water can get deep. We want to walk on the ledges near the tunnel walls.'

Valen stepped onto the ridge and laid his left hand on the wall's cold, wet bricks. They tiptoed down the sewer till they reached a four-way crossroads. Chloe turned left, which led them further west.

Valen frowned as his hand touched a smooth wall. 'This doesn't look like a sewer wall? It's smooth and not bricked.'

'That wall was part of the old town,' Chloe said. 'It was called Farmacre, as I understand it. They built Fairacre on top of it.'

'Never understood the name Fairacre,' Valen said. 'Farmacre makes more sense.'

'They chose the name Fairacre because every man got to choose a wife. It was fair for men, not for women.'

Valen's low growl echoed through the tunnels. They continued walking until they hit another crossroads. Chloe turned right and continued walking north. The stink of the sewers disappeared the deeper they travelled.

'We are entering the parts of the sewers that run outside the town of Fairacre,' Chloe said. 'We are under the western wheat fields.'

'This place is massive,' Valen said.

Chloe smiled over her shoulder. 'Farmacre was a lot bigger than Fairacre.'

'What was that?' Valen said, stopping and tilting his head. 'Did you hear that?'

Chloe knelt and placed a finger on her lips. 'Guards. Do you think they followed us?'

'I don't think so,' Valen said. 'They are coming from another direction. I think they are scouting.'

Chloe stood and continued down the tunnel. 'Let's keep moving.'

A few minutes later, Valen stopped. 'I can hear voices.'

'It's the children,' Chloe said, increasing her speed. 'We need to get there and warn them about these guards.'

They turned another corner and Valen froze at all the eyes staring back at him. Chloe let go a soft whistle. The young girls stood in unison, collected their things, and started walking.

'That's it?' Valen said. 'You just move?'

'We are always on the move,' Chloe said. 'It's the only way we don't get caught.'

'This is horrible,' Valen muttered. 'I cannot understand it. Disgusting that young children should have to live like this. I really don't understand it.'

'Hello, Valen,' Naomi said, appearing out of the darkness. 'I would say I am surprised to see you, but I am not. Young Chloe here is not one for following the rules.'

Valen turned a slight pink. 'You don't say.'

Naomi raised an eyebrow.

'I felt it would be a good idea if Valen saw how we lived,' Chloe said, elbowing him in the side. 'I wanted him to see how these young girls live.'

'Chloe wants me to go back into Fairacre,' Valen said.

Naomi opened her mouth, then closed it as voices sounded deep down in the tunnels.

'We need to move,' Chloe whispered.

Naomi disappeared into the darkness and reappeared at the head of the train of girls. The group walked in silence, weaving through the different tunnels. Eventually, they stopped in a large open area.

'It is amazing how everyone keeps so quiet,' Valen said.

'We do this all day,' Chloe said. 'It's a pattern. We just walk around in circles.'

'Boo,' Gracie said, jumping out of the darkness and wrapping her arms around Valen's neck.

Valen wrapped his massive arms around her and hugged back. 'Hello, missy. I have missed you.'

'Ow,' Gracie said. 'Careful, the ribs.'

'So sorry,' Valen said, pulling away. 'How are you?'

'Tired of being down in this hellhole,' Gracie said. 'I want to go topside.'

'When those ribs are fine, you can go,' Chloe said.

Little Henry jumped out of Valen's pocket and scuttled over to Gracie. He danced around in a circle and clacked his jaws.

Valen sighed. 'Even my beasties are disowning me.'

'Hello, Little Henry,' Gracie said, while scratching the top of his head.

Voices sounded down the tunnel. Another whisper from Naomi. Everyone stood and continued walking through the maze of tunnels.

'This is ridiculous,' Valen said. 'How do you ever sleep?'

'It will stop soon,' Chloe said. 'The guards search once or twice a week, then they go missing. It gives us a bit of time to sleep and eat.'

They turned left down another tunnel and continued walking. A few minutes later, Naomi brought them to a halt.

'We can relax now,' Chloe said.

Valen sat down next to Gracie and bumped her with his shoulder. 'What's news?'

Gracie grinned at Little Henry as he ran over her hand. 'Absolutely no news what with being down here. I heard you were in jail.'

'That is a story for another time, young Gracie,' Chloe said. 'Valen needs to rest. Can you go and get him a blanket if we have any spare?'

'Of course,' Gracie said, disappearing into the darkness.

Naomi walked back over and sat. 'It is good to see you, old friend.'

'I would say the same,' Valen said. 'But I am appalled at these living conditions.'

'We had a nice place in the sewers before the guards found it,' Naomi said. 'A few rooms where we could burn candles to give light. We could even light a fire as the ventilation was good.'

Valen peered down the tunnel. 'Some of these girls are so young. What of their parents?'

'People from all regions abandon them outside the gates of Fairacre,' Chloe said. 'They know that nobody will ask them questions.'

'Heartbreaking,' Valen said. 'And the older girls? Where do they come from?'

'Men order them from the schools and then abandon them when they are not what they expect,' Chloe said. 'Some of these girls have incredible skills, but they cannot use them down here.'

Valen thought of the girls walking past the barn.

'It has been happening for decades,' Chloe said. 'It is now accepted as normal. Even the abandoned girls think it was their fault, so they just accept it.'

With a long breath, Valen lowered his head into his hands.

'Come now,' Chloe said. 'It is time you get some rest. We should be safe for a while.'

Gracie returned with a rough blanket. Valen stretched out on the lip of the sewer's edge and placed his head on Chloe's lap. Within seconds, he was fast asleep.

CHAPTER 7
A NEW HOME

A hand snaked over Valen's mouth.

'Wake up,' Chloe whispered into his ear.

'What is it?' he mumbled, his eyes snapping open.

'They have found us,' Chloe said.

Valen pulled back the blanket and got to his feet. Chloe placed a finger on her lips and jabbed a thumb down the tunnel.

'Where are the others?' Valen said into her ear.

'They have gone the opposite direction,' Chloe said. 'We are going to stay behind and keep the guards busy until Naomi finds a new place to hide.'

'Time to get to work, you two,' Valen said, opening his pockets. 'Jay, you stay here. You are too loud.'

Little Henry scuttled off down the sewer. Sia slithered into the water trickling along the tunnel floor.

Chloe, Valen, and Chloe's team moved in the same direction Naomi had gone. In the distance, they could hear the guards' footsteps and chatter bouncing off the tunnel walls.

'We are near the surface,' Valen said. 'See these roots on the walls? They are from the western forest.'

Chloe ran a hand along the thick vine-like roots snaking along the sewer wall. They continued walking until they came to a crossroads.

'Which way did they go?' Valen said.

'Straight on,' Alexa said. 'But it sounds like they are coming back.'

Gracie appeared out of the darkness. 'It's a dead end. We need to go a different way.'

'I will check this way,' Alexa said, pointing to the right. 'Come with me, Gracie.'

'Chloe and I will check the left tunnel,' Valen said, grabbing her by the hand.

They snaked along the winding tunnel of the dark sewers. A minute later, they entered a small chamber with a low roof.

'It's a dead end,' Chloe said. 'Let's get back and see what Alexa has found.'

Valen retraced their steps towards the crossroads. Halfway along the tunnel, Valen stopped and squinted at one of the tunnel walls.

'What is it?' Chloe said. 'What can you see?'

'There are more vines here than usual,' Valen said, reaching through the vines to find the wall.

Chloe snaked her hand through the vines and touched the wall. 'It's not brick. It's smooth and cold.'

Valen followed Chloe's hand. 'It's steel,' he said. 'Move out of the way for a second, please, love.'

Chloe took a step back.

'Let me get some of these smaller roots out of the way,' Valen said. 'We need to find the place where this steel wall meets the brick wall.'

A shout echoed through the sewers.

'I think they have found us,' Chloe said, her forehead creasing in concern. 'I need to go and help.'

'Bring them up here,' Valen said.

'It's a dead end down here,' Chloe said. 'We will have nowhere to go.'

'I think it's a dead end all three ways except where the guards are,' Valen said. 'And I also think this metal wall is actually a door.'

Chloe's eyebrows shot into her locs. 'You think?'

'Yes,' Valen said. 'I just need to find the end. Go and get the sewer rats.'

'I will be back,' Chloe said, disappearing into the darkness.

Valen tore at the roots until he could run his hand along the steel wall. He followed the steel until his hand hit the brick. He fumbled around, looking for a handle. After not finding anything, he knelt and ran his finger along the bottom of the wall. He struck a round object. 'Wheels,' Valen said. 'Of course. It's a sliding door.' In the distance, he heard the children's footsteps coming his way. Valen felt the door in the other direction until he touched the wall's rough bricks. He grabbed the side of the steel door and shoved gently. It rocked on its wheels.

'They have found us and we don't have anywhere to go,' Gracie said, appearing out of the darkness.

'Help me with this, will you?' Valen said, as he moved some roots out of the way. 'We need to make space to move this door.'

'There is a door here?' Gracie said. 'It looks like a wall.'

'Yes, it's a sliding door,' Valen said. 'Help me get these roots out of the way, will you?'

Gracie tore away some of the smaller roots.

'This side,' Valen said, moving to the end of the steel door. 'We need to give the door space to move.'

Gracie moved over and tugged at the roots. With a crack, the roots let go of the wall.

Naomi appeared out of the darkness.

'Where is Chloe?' Valen said.

'She is hiding at the crossroads to engage with the guards,' Naomi said.

'Help me get this door open,' Valen said. 'Quickly as we can.'

Naomi, Gracie, and a few of the children moved the roots aside. Valen kept trying the door, but pieces kept catching. After a minute, the door budged.

'It's a big room,' Gracie said, looking through the gap. 'It doesn't look like a sewer.'

'Come on,' Valen said. 'We need to get this open.'

Everyone doubled their efforts until the door opened just enough for people to squeeze through.

'Get everyone inside,' Valen said. 'I am going to get Chloe.'

'Be careful,' Gracie said.

Valen used the wall to guide him through the sewer. He stopped and listened. In the distance, the clash of swords echoed down the tunnels. Valen let go of the wall and ran towards the fighting. At the crossroads, Alexa stood with a short sword drawn.

'Where is Chloe?' Valen said.

'Fighting a guard up the tunnel,' Alexa said. 'She is holding them off.'

'Go back that way and look for Naomi,' Valen said. 'They have found a place to hide.'

'What about Chloe?' Alexa said.

'I will get her,' Valen said. 'Go. You can do nothing more here.'

Alexa jogged down the tunnel.

Valen ran towards the fighting. He followed a kink in the tunnel, then skidded to a halt. In the middle of a small chamber, Chloe knelt with her hands tied behind her back and a cloth bound through her mouth.

'What do we do with her?' a guard said.

'The Captain will want her,' the other said.

A roar of anger exploded from Valen. He charged into the guards with fists and feet swinging in every direction. The first guard didn't even see what was coming before he crumpled to the ground. A moment later, the second guard fell face-first into the floor.

Chloe mumbled through the cloth. Valen gave the second guard another kick to make sure he was unconscious. He then moved over to Chloe and undid her gag.

'Valen, your side,' Chloe said

Valen looked down and saw the thick blood dripping from his side. He lifted his shirt and touched the deep gash that ran across his hip and onto his back. He dropped his shirt over the wound and undid Chloe's bonds.

Chloe stood and caught Valen just as he fell to a knee.

'I am OK,' Valen said through gritted teeth. 'Let's get back to the door.'

Chloe threw Valen's arm over her shoulder and pulled him to his feet. The two of them stumbled along the sewer pipe towards the crossroads.

Behind them, a guard screamed in horror.

'My beasties are causing havoc,' Valen said, grinning.

At the crossroads they turned left and moved down the tunnel. In the darkness, Valen saw Gracie's head looking out from the door.

'Over here,' Gracie said, waving a hand.

Chloe and Valen stumbled to the door.

'Here, help him,' Chloe said, lifting Valen's arm off her neck.

Gracie reached out to grab his hand.

'In you go,' Valen said, dodging Gracie's hand and shoving Chloe through the door.

'What are you doing?' Chloe hissed.

Valen slid the door until it was nearly closed. He looked Chloe in the eye. 'I love you,' he said.

'Valen, get in here,' Chloe said, reaching for him.

'Stay there Chloe,' Valen said, then closed the door.

A few fists pounded the metal door and then it turned silent. Valen smiled. 'Time to have some fun with these guards.'

'Where did they go?' a guard said down the tunnel.

Valen pulled himself to his full height and walked towards the guards. 'Hello, boys,' he said, walking out into the light.

The guards drew their swords. Valen pounced with a roar, knocking them to the ground. He turned down the tunnel and hobbled as fast as he could away from the sewer rats. The guards, getting back to their feet, gave chase. Valen turned down as many tunnels as he could. Left, right, right and left. The following guards slowly caught up to him. A misty haze filled Valen's sight. The loss of blood took its toll. He dropped to a knee.

Sia and Little Henry slithered and scuttled over.

'Get out of here,' Valen hissed. 'You too, Jay.'

Jay buzzed out of Valen's pocket and disappeared down a tunnel. Sia slithered away. Little Henry clapped his jaws, then scuttled away.

'Here he is!' a guard shouted.

Valen fell to his other knee. The tunnel swirled around him. He looked up at the approaching guard and grinned.

'What are you smiling at, outsider?' the guard said.

'You have lost them,' Valen said. 'They have escaped to the west. You are rubbish at your job.'

The guard snarled.

Valen closed his eyes just as the pommel of the guard's sword connected with his face.

.   .   .

101

Valen blinked. Pain throbbed through his body. He looked down at his side to see thick white bandages wrapped around his torso. More pain stabbed through him as he tried to sit up. Voices of guards sitting nearby became clearer as the rest of his senses kicked in.

'He is waking up,' a guard said. 'Unbelievable.'

'Best call the Captain,' the other guard said.

Valen grimaced as the cell's metal doors screeched open and then closed. He ran his tongue over his dry, cracked lips.

'I guess you be wanting some water, outsider?' the guard said.

'Yes, please,' Valen whispered.

'Going to wait for the Captain,' the guard said. 'Not going to be doing anything I shouldn't be doing before he gets here.'

A croak came out of Valen's mouth as he tried to speak. On the third attempt, he gave up trying to say anything. The metal doors of the cell opened and closed.

'Well, well, well,' the Captain said. 'It is truly remarkable that you are alive, outsider.'

'Looks like he wants some water, boss,' the guard said.

'Well, give it to him then,' the Captain said, cuffing the guard around the back of his head. 'We need to question him.'

'Yes, sir,' the guard said, scuttling away.

Valen's cell door sprang open. The Captain walked in holding a small wooden stool. He dumped it next to Valen's bed and sat on it. The guard hurried in with water.

'Hold it for him,' the Captain said.

The guard dribbled some of the water into Valen's mouth.

'Think you can talk now, big guy?' the Captain said.

'How long have I been out?' Valen whispered.

'Days,' the Captain said. 'We didn't know if you were going to make it.'

'Where am I?' Valen said.

'You know where you are,' the Captain said. 'Your second home. The lovely jail underneath the town hall.'

'I need more water,' Valen whispered.

'I don't care what you want. Where are those filthy sewer rats?' the Captain said.

Valen swallowed hard.

The Captain sighed and waved his hand. The guard dribbled a few more splashes of water into Valen's mouth.

'So where are they, outsider?' the Captain said.

'West,' Valen whispered.

'What was that?' the Captain said, leaning in.

'They went west,' Valen said. 'To the girl's land. Where the black people live.'

The Captain sat back and folded his arms. 'Even now you lie here half-dead and you try to protect them.'

'They went west,' Valen said. 'Ask your guards.'

'We searched the sewers for openings they could use to escape,' the Captain said. 'And we found nothing.'

Valen chuckled. 'You didn't look hard enough. There are many ways out of that sewer. Even you know that.'

The Captain stared at Valen for a minute. With a sigh, he stood. 'Get some rest, outsider. Hargreaves is busy deciding what to do with you.'

'I want to speak to him,' Valen said, his voice cracking.

'Hargreaves would never come down here,' the Captain said with a smirk. 'He is way too upper class for the prisons. Your best hope is to get better and go and see him.'

Valen closed his eyes. The cell door slammed shut. Darkness swept over him.

. . .

Valen woke up in darkness. He wrapped his arms around himself. His shivering rattled his teeth. Sweat poured off his face and body. The world around him swirled.

'Got the fever, he has,' a guard said.

Valen opened his eyes and tried to focus on the guard. The world swirled. He closed his eyes and let the darkness take over.

'Drink, outsider,' the guard said, nudging Valen. 'You need to get some liquid down you.'

'I am hot,' Valen said. 'My veins feel like they are on fire.'

'That be the fever,' the guard said. 'Nothing I can do for you. Drink.'

Valen closed his eyes.

'Open your mouth and drink,' the guard said, nudging him.

Valen opened his eyes and took a sip of water.

'How is he doing?' the Captain said.

'It is a miracle he is still alive,' a guard said. 'This fever should have killed him a day ago.'

'Keep making him drink,' the Captain said.

'Yes, sir,' the guard said.

Valen grimaced at the squeal of the big jail door.

A day later, Valen opened his eyes. For the first time in what seemed like forever, everything swam into focus. The pain in his side was now just a dull ache. He moved his legs and felt a throb of pain down his side. With a sharp intake of breath, he pulled himself up and swung his feet off the bed.

'Sure you ready for that?' the Captain said, with his hands on his hips.

Valen looked at the Captain and grinned. 'It's good to see you too, Captain.'

The Captain snorted. 'It's a wonder to see you alive, outsider.

Most men would have died from that wound. You must have an angel looking over you.'

'It doesn't feel too bad,' Valen said, placing his hand on top of the bandage and pressing on it.

'It is a mystery,' the Captain said. 'The doctor came down here and stitched you up. Made a right mess of it because he said he cared little for outsiders. Next morning, though, someone else had restitched you.'

Valen smiled at the Captain.

'So you know who did it?' the Captain said. 'A sewer rat who came through the sewers?'

'Your guards would be terrible at their job if that was the case, Captain,' Valen said.

'Don't get me started,' the Captain said, glancing at the guard who sat staring into space. 'So who did it?'

'I have no idea,' Valen said, thinking of Little Henry.

The Captain let out a dramatic sigh. 'You are a mystery, outsider.'

'I don't wish to be an outsider anymore,' Valen said quietly.

The jail fell silent. Even the guard looked back down at Valen.

'What was that?' the Captain said, leaning in. 'What did you say?'

Valen looked up at the Captain. 'I have made my choice. I do not wish to be an outsider any longer.'

The Captain looked at his two guards then back at Valen. 'Why the change of heart?'

'Let's just say, a near-death experience changes a man, Captain,' Valen said, as he gingerly pressed his side.

'Hmm,' the Captain said, placing his hands behind his back. 'This I know to be very true, my dear boy.'

'Can I see Hargreaves?' Valen said.

'Well, after this change of heart,' the Captain said, 'I will update Hargreaves. Maybe he will reconsider your position.'

'Does that mean he is going to buy a wife?' a guard said, looking at the Captain. 'There will be a new set of girls coming down next season.'

Valen cast his mind back to the girls walking past the big red barn. He concentrated on keeping his face neutral.

'So, outsider,' the Captain said, watching Valen carefully. 'Are you going to be buying a wife?'

'I will be, yes,' Valen said. 'But I want to stay in my shop.'

The Captain rocked back on his heels. 'You will need to buy a house in the northern district. That is part of the terms, Valen.'

Valen nodded. 'I will have both places. Sometimes I need to work late into the night, so I want a guarantee I can also stay in my shop.'

'Well, what a turn of events,' the Captain said. 'And here I was, getting the hanging noose ready.'

'When can I see Hargreaves?' Valen said.

'I will take you to him tomorrow once I have spoken to him,' the Captain said. 'Get some rest, outsider.'

Valen lay back down on the bed. He interlaced his fingers behind his head and smiled up at the cell ceiling. He closed his eyes and drifted in and out of sleep. Every time he woke, a picture of Chloe's face played across his mind. The sun set, leaving the jail in quiet darkness. For the first time in a while, Valen fell into a deep sleep.

'Let's go, outsider,' the Captain said, unlocking the cell door.

Valen's eyes fluttered open. He swung his legs off the side of his bed and grunted at the sharp stab of pain. With both hands, he pushed himself off the bed. He steadied himself by stretching out his arms.

'I can see your ribs,' the guard said. 'Nothing but skin and bone.'

'That's the fever for you,' the Captain said. 'It will reduce the biggest man to a skeleton.'

Valen looked at his hands and raised an eyebrow at his thin, bony fingers. He lifted his shirt and shook his head at the bones of his hips.

'Going to take you a while to get back to being yourself again,' the Captain said. 'Follow me.'

'No restraints?' Valen said, holding out his wrists.

As the Captain walked away, he chuckled over his shoulder. 'The only thing you might hurt right now is a fly. Come on, let's go.'

Valen shuffled through the jail. The Captain walked slowly so Valen could keep up. At the exit, Valen held onto the railing to walk up the stairs. The sunlight hit him square in the face. His eyes stung and watered.

'You need help?' the Captain said, reaching out a hand.

Valen shook his head. 'Thank you, Captain, but I would prefer walking out of here on my two feet.'

'Good man,' the Captain said with a smile.

They made their way up the stairs and around the town hall. People peered at Valen with a look of worry and confusion.

'They don't know who you are,' the Captain said.

'Hardly anyone knew me before,' Valen said.

'They knew you, outsider,' the Captain said. 'They would just get into trouble if they ever spoke to you.'

Valen breathed heavily as he battled his way up the stairs to the town hall entrance. At the top, the Captain held open the door for him. Valen welcomed the cool air of the town hall. The two of them slowly made their way to the mayor's office. The Captain knocked.

'Come in,' Mr Hargreaves said.

Valen and the Captain walked in.

Mr Hargreaves stared at Valen. 'You are skin and bone.'

Valen gave Mr Hargreaves a thin-lipped smile.

'Sit,' Mr Hargreaves said, pointing to a chair.

'I am here to say I want to be part of Fairacre,' Valen said as he sank into the comfortable chair.

'I have heard from the Captain,' Mr Hargreaves said, standing and walking around the desk. 'Why the change of heart?'

'As I mentioned to the Captain, we only get one chance at life and I want to live it properly.'

Mr Hargreaves looked at the Captain with a raised eyebrow.

The Captain shrugged his shoulders.

'You know what this means, Valen,' Mr Hargreaves said.

'I must choose a wife,' Valen said, while keeping a neutral face.

'Yes,' Mr Hargreaves said. 'And move to the northern district.'

'It will take time to save money for a place in the northern district,' Valen said. 'I request I stay in my shop with my new wife until I have earned the funds to purchase this place.'

'We can offer you a loan?' Mr Hargreaves said, moving back around his desk. 'It is a common practice.'

Valen held up a hand. 'I wish to pay my own way. But thank you kindly.'

The Captain cleared his throat.

'What is it?' Mr Hargreaves said.

'I think our young sewer-rat lover here is up to something,' the Captain said.

Mr Hargreaves frowned at Valen. 'I think he may be up to something, but we have to give him the benefit of the doubt. Any news on the sewer rats?'

'Nothing,' the Captain said. 'They have gone missing completely. The outsider here says they have all gone west.'

Mr Hargreaves looked at Valen. 'I do not think the western people will accept them. They are a people who like to keep to themselves.'

Valen stared at Mr Hargreaves with unblinking eyes. He bit the inside of his cheek to stop himself from saying anything.

Mr Hargreaves picked up a pen and bounced it on his chin. 'I am inclined to accept your request,' he said. 'However, you will still need to be punished for your treason towards Fairacre.'

'A hanging then, sir?' the Captain said, with a tilt of his head.

'Not everyone deserves the noose, Captain,' Mr Hargreaves said. 'Plus, how would he be able to buy a house in the northern district if we hanged him?'

The Captain rolled his eyes at Valen.

'Oh, that was a joke,' Mr Hargreaves said with a shake of the head.

'Bravo,' the Captain said with a deadpan face.

Mr Hargreaves turned to Valen. 'For your treason, Valen, I commit you to jail for one season cycle. We will release you on the first spring day of the new season.'

'A winter in the Fairacre jail,' the Captain said. 'Few survive.'

'He survived the fever,' Mr Hargreaves said. 'No reason for him not to survive a winter.'

Valen looked Mr Hargreaves straight in the eye. 'If you think I deserve this punishment, then I accept.'

'Take him away,' Mr Hargreaves said, waving a hand. 'Make sure he gets fed and has the correct treatment, Captain. I do not wish to see a future citizen pass away because of our negligence.'

'Yes, sir,' the Captain said, grabbing Valen's elbow. 'Come on. Let's get you back to your new home.'

Valen followed the Captain out into the town square. The bright sun of the last few days of summer warmed Valen's face. He looked up towards the sun and took in the life-giving heat.

'We can wait here for a second,' the Captain said.

Valen gave the Captain a nod as he peered towards the sun with his eyes closed. He breathed in deeply, knowing this would be the last time he felt the sun or breathed in fresh air for a full season.

'I am going to continue to look for the sewer rats,' the Captain said. 'I know they are still here. We will expose your trickery, Valen.'

Valen smiled at the sun. After a minute, he lowered his head and scanned the rooftops of Fairacre. A flash of black material disappeared into an alley.

'Let's go,' the Captain said, guiding Valen down the stairs. 'Time to get you settled.'

Fifteen minutes later, Valen jumped as the Captain slammed the cell door. He moved over to the newly covered straw bed and stretched out along it. He looked out of the one tiny window and steeled himself for the icy winter about to hit the town of Fairacre.

CHAPTER 8
ANOTHER ONE SAVED

The tip-tap of little metal feet woke Valen. A sliver of moonlight pierced through the window of his cell. His breath created plumes of hot steam as he lay curled up in a ball. The aching in his feet and hands from the cold never went away. His teeth chattered.

Little Henry appeared on the floor below Valen, where he dropped a small piece of paper. Valen picked up the paper and clutched it to his chest. Little Henry scuttled off into a crack in the wall.

The next morning, Valen sat on his bed and waited patiently for the sun to creep over the sky. Just after midday, a single beam of light shone through the window. Valen grabbed a small stool and placed it in the centre of his cell. He sat with his back to the guards and opened up the slip of paper.

My dear Valen,

I hope you are OK. We are settling into our new home. Small adventures onto the surface for food. Stay strong. I will see you soon.

All my love.
Chloe.

Valen popped the piece of paper into his mouth, chewed it, and swallowed. He stood and began his daily pacing to keep warm.

The guard grinned up at him. 'Got a little extra bread for you today, outsider.'

Valen inclined his head. 'Always a treat from you, my good man.'

The guard pulled out his knife and continued whittling away at a small block of wood, which he kept stored in his pocket.

'Any news from above?' Valen said. 'Any Fairacre news or gossip?'

'It is quiet,' the guard said. 'The cold has gripped the town, making everyone stay indoors. The Captain has slowed down his searching for the sewer rats.'

'Oh, has he?' Valen said. 'Other things on his mind?'

'I think so,' the guard said. 'Mr Hargreaves has been going to the City of Lynn more regularly. The Captain has been running the City in his absence.'

Valen walked back to his bed. 'Thanks for the chat, my good man.'

'Anytime,' the guard said, as he pulled a small sliver from the block of wood. 'Anytime.'

A month later, Valen grabbed a small piece of paper from Little Henry and hid it in his sock. He curled up into a ball to slow the shivering. The dull moonlight twinkled as the snow continued to fall.

At midday, Valen pulled the stool into the middle of the cell and waited for the sunbeam to shine through the window. He pulled the piece of paper from his sock and unrolled it.

It is me, Gracie,

I am going mad down here. I miss you and the shop really badly. I have made a decision. I am going to the west on an adventure and I am so excited. Don't hate me for leaving you. I will be back.

Love you, miss you, Gracie.

Valen popped the note into his mouth and swallowed. He scraped the stool back and began his backwards-and-forwards pacing.

After an hour, the enormous steel door rattled open, then slammed shut. 'Well, well, well,' Dec said. 'You are looking slightly better, outsider.'

'We must be feeding him too much,' Jon said, kicking out at the young guard.

Dec snatched at the young guard's block of wood.

'Leave him be, gentleman,' Valen growled.

Dec chuckled. 'Whatever, outsider. How are you feeling?'

Valen continued his walking. 'Cold and tired of this place. How are you two gentlemen doing?'

'I beat Dec at dice,' Jon said, swelling out his chest. 'First time in a long time.'

'Well done,' Valen said with a smirk. 'Good of Dec to let someone else win sometimes.'

Dec snorted. 'So we hear you are going to be buying a wife when we release you?'

'I am going to take my time, gentleman,' Valen said. 'But, yes, I shall be buying a wife.'

'Mr Hargreaves seems to visit the schools on the cliffs more and more these days,' Jon said. 'Maybe he is looking for a wife for you.'

Valen stopped walking. 'Why would Mr Hargreaves be visiting the schools?'

Dec shrugged. 'No idea. Maybe checking up on how they are being trained for us?'

Valen continued his pacing.

'Give me that,' Dec said, snatching at the block of wood again.

'When are you two getting married?' Valen said, to distract Dec from the young guard.

'Aww, you know,' Jon said. 'Haven't found the right one, me.'

'Don't earn that much money being gate guards,' Dec said. 'We don't have many girls to choose from.'

Valen upped his pacing.

'I hope that won't affect the wife you choose for me, gentlemen?' Valen said, his smile widening.

'Of course not,' Jon and Dec said at the same time.

'Gentlemen,' Valen said, walking up to the cell bars. 'Keep an eye out for any market stalls that come available. I think I am going to open my own arts and crafts stall.'

'OK, outsider,' Jon said. 'I will see if we can get one close to us.'

'Even better,' Valen said. 'We can talk all day when nobody is around.'

Dec and Jon both chuckled. 'See you later, outsider.'

Valen watched the two guards leave the jail. He smiled as the door slammed shut.

'Thank you,' the guard said. 'Those two are bullies.'

'Oh, they sure are,' Valen said under his breath.

. . .

The sound of songbirds brought in the first signs of spring. The snow and the biting cold of the nights were no more. Valen lay on his straw bed with his hands behind his head.

Clack-clack went Little Henry's jaws. Valen picked up the tiny note on his chest. At midday, he pulled the stool to the centre of the cell and waited for the sunbeam to hit the right spot.

My Love,

    Gracie has left for the west. Our new home is taking shape. Saved twins, Jen and Gem, from Donte, and oh boy, can they cook! I have my own room! Your release is soon, and I cannot wait. Stay strong, love.

    Chloe.

Valen popped the note in his mouth, chewed, and swallowed.

'Food time,' the guard said, pulling a stool up to the bars.

Valen pulled his stool up and sat facing the guard. He picked up a piece of bread and slathered it with some butter. 'Very good,' he said, chewing hungrily.

'Your time is nearly up,' the guard said with a look of sadness.

'What have they got in store for you next then?' Valen said.

'Delegates from the City of Lynn have been more frequent,' the guard said. 'I will do guard duty for when the visitors sleep.'

'You have a unique ability to stay wide awake during the night,' Valen said.

The guard chuckled. 'It's called sleeping with my eyes open. What about you?'

'I am going to rebuild my life,' Valen said. 'My shop is waiting for me and I wish to open a stall in the market.'

'They haven't touched your shop,' the guard said.

Valen raised an eyebrow. 'They haven't? I would have thought someone would have ransacked it.'

'It seems the Captain and Hargreaves made sure everyone left it alone,' the guard said. 'What else you going to get up to?'

'Obviously, buy myself a bride,' Valen said with a grin.

The guard nodded. 'That is good news.'

'Good enough for your report back to the Captain?' Valen said.

The guard inclined his head. 'As long as it's the truth?'

'It is,' Valen said, leaning back and wiping his mouth. 'My love is arts and crafts and someone told me there are women in the schools on the cliffs who enjoy the same activity. I will make sure I get a list of who they are.'

'Good man,' the guard said, scraping his chair back.

Valen lay back on his bed and placed his hands behind his head. He closed his eyes and brought up images of Chloe.

'It's time,' the Captain said, marching up to Valen's cell. 'Are you ready, outsider?'

'You won't need to call me outsider for long,' Valen said.

The Captain unlocked the door and stood aside. Valen stepped out and waited for the Captain to close the cell.

'Follow me,' the Captain said.

Valen followed the Captain through the jail and up the stairs into the spring sunlight. At the top, Valen lifted his head and took in a long breath.

'See you around,' the Captain said as he jogged around the town hall.

'Is that it?' Valen said.

'What were you expecting, outsider?' the Captain said. 'A fanfare?'

Valen shrugged. 'I guess not. See you around, Captain.'

The Captain disappeared around the town hall. Valen looked down at his torn brown clothes. The frayed edges of his shirt and trousers made him look like he had been living on the streets all his life. A slithering sound came from the grass near him. Valen knelt and extended his arm. 'Hello, Sia,' he said as the snake climbed up. Jay suddenly appeared, buzzing angrily. Valen walked around the town hall and entered the square. People turned their noses up and gave him a wide berth. He continued down the east–west road and turned south into the weaving district. The familiar thump, thump of the weaving loom was music to his ears. He wound down the roads to the southern wall. At the single light flickering on and off, Valen stopped and looked at his shop. The outside chairs lay stacked on the table. The hanging baskets contained dead plants. Someone had cracked a window from top to bottom. Valen walked up and tried the shop door-handle. The bell tinkled as he opened the door. A smell of vinegar struck his nose. He walked into the shop and stopped. Someone had been keeping the shop clean. Valen walked around the counter and through the aisles to the office.

'Welcome home,' Chloe said, her leg bouncing off the armrest of the couch.

Valen sank to the couch and let out a long sigh. 'I should have known you would be here.'

'Good to be out?' Chloe said.

A lump caught in Valen's throat. He brought his feet up onto the couch and lowered his head onto Chloe's lap. As her hand stroked his head, he let the tears soak the couch's brown fabric. The power of freedom coursed through his body.

'Get out of my way!' Valen shouted.

Little Henry danced in a circle, then jumped from the office desk onto the couch.

'You are a nuisance,' Valen said, waving a finger at Little Henry. The spider lifted two legs and waved them at Valen. Little Jay dive-bombed Henry, then flew around the office at great speed. Sia lay curled up in the desk's corner.

'What are your plans for today?' Chloe said, walking out of the kitchen and handing Valen a mug of tea.

'It seems Dec and Jon have a vacant stall ready for me to look at,' Valen said.

'Valen the tradesman,' Chloe said, wagging her eyebrows. 'I like it.'

Valen chuckled. 'Better than Valen the spy?'

'Ohh, now that is even better,' Chloe said with a wide smile. 'Do you get to slink in the shadows and listen to everyone's darkest secrets?'

'I think you guys have skulking in the shadows covered,' Valen said, smiling.

Chloe sat on the couch. 'The new home you found for us in the sewers is a lot bigger than we first thought. It seems it's the actual town of Farmacre, and the metal door is an exit into the old sewers.'

'That is great to hear,' Valen said. 'But now we need to keep it safe from the Captain.'

'Something has distracted him all summer,' Chloe said. 'Something to do with the City of Lynn. Teachers. Finishing schools. Well, those are the rumours, anyway.'

'At least that will give you a little more freedom,' Valen said.

Chloe took another sip of her tea. 'We have rescued several girls from Donte.'

Valen sat back in his office chair. 'And I assume you cannot go and get all of them for fear of bringing attention to yourself?'

'Yes,' Chloe said. 'Even now, some eyebrows are being raised.'

'Leave that with me,' Valen said. 'I will send a few distraction messages through Dec and Jon.'

Chloe stood and sat on Valen's lap. She curled her arms around his neck.

'I thought about you every day when I was in jail,' Valen said.

'I thought about you occasionally,' Chloe said.

'Hey,' Valen said.

Chloe chuckled.

The doorbell at the front of the shop tinkled. Chloe jumped off Valen and hid in the shadows. With her back to the counter stood a young girl.

'Can I help you?' Valen said.

The young girl's long, red hair rippled as she turned around. 'Hi, yes, my name is Janie, and I am looking for these items for the household,' she said, handing Valen a list.

'Certainly,' Valen said, peering at the list. 'And which lucky household is the receiver of all of this?'

'Donte's household,' Janie said with a forced smile.

Valen looked at the list, then at the girl. 'Donte, you say?'

Janie looked down at her hands. 'Yes, sir, Donte.'

'And how is it going at Donte's?' Valen said, moving between the shelves and collecting the items.

Janie forced another smile.

'Hi, Janie,' Chloe said, walking out from behind the shelves. 'Don't be afraid. I just want to talk.'

Janie looked between Valen and Chloe.

'I will make some tea,' Valen said, walking into his office.

Chloe smiled at Janie. 'So tell me, Janie, have you heard of the sewer rats?'

NEXT UP...

Miles and the Soldier

The front door swung open. The icy blast of air hit Miles full in the face.

For the first time in months, a smile played across his lips.

Freedom.

Miles knows his life changed when the Lady's sword cut deep into his back. He knows he'll never achieve his lifelong dream.

Then a stab of joyous pain slices down his leg. With renewed hope, Miles leaves behind the shackles of Dr Viktor's house and travels east, to the training grounds of the Queen's Guard.

Will Miles get the chance to compete for a place? And will they accept him in the warrior's holy ground of Battleacre?

The Acre Story follows Miles's journey through the eastern lands as our epic fantasy continues.

AUTHOR REQUEST

Hello,

Thank you for taking the time to read **Valen and the Beasts**. It is the first prequel novella of Juno and the Lady. I will be releasing more Juno novellas in the months to come.

If you have a moment, I would really appreciate a review on either Amazon or Goodreads. The reviews help us indie authors a great deal.

Please consider joining my mailing list where I will keep you up to date with book release dates, news and upcoming events. https://gjkemp.co.uk/mailing-list/

Again, thank you for spending your precious time reading my books.

Take care,
G.J.

ABOUT THE AUTHOR

A nomad at heart, GJ has lived in nine countries across Africa, Europe and the Middle East. His career has included working as a Divemaster in The Red Sea, a zookeeper in Israel, and a proofreader in Sweden. Born with cerebral palsy, GJ has spent a lifetime trying to tie his shoelaces while standing up in the hope of not falling over. It is a constant challenge, but sometimes he occasionally succeeds.

Finding the love for writing later in life, GJ spends most of his free time going for walks and dreaming of story ideas. He hopes to one day have a small place on the oceanfront where he can walk his dogs on the beach.

For more information please visit gjkemp.co.uk

facebook.com/gavin.kemp.92505

twitter.com/kemp_gj

instagram.com/gjkempauthor

linkedin.com/in/g-j-kemp-4a76b03

bookbub.com/profile/g-j-kemp

Printed in Great Britain
by Amazon

32358119R00078